ALIEN CITADEL

Douglas Hill is a Canadian who has lived in Britain for several years, where he is now literary editor of the weekly *Tribune.* He is the author of more than twenty non-fiction books and the editor of five anthologies of science fiction and fantasy for adults and one for children. In the many years of his involvement with science fiction he has been a reviewer, magazine staff editor, publishers' consultant, and author of numerous articles and short stories. His previous science fiction for children, the Last Legionary quartet of novels, has been called 'the best kids' SF of the last decade' (*Books for Keeps*) and 'the best thing since Dan Dare and Mekon' (*The Times Literary Supplement*).

Alien Citadel completes the story of Finn Ferral the hero of *The Huntsman* and *Warriors of the Wasteland.*

Also by Douglas Hill in Piccolo

WARRIORS OF THE WASTELAND
THE HUNTSMAN
ALIEN WORLDS (anthology)
The Last Legionary Series
GALACTIC WARLORD
DEATHWING OVER VEYNAA
DAY OF THE STARWIND
PLANET OF THE WARLORD
YOUNG LEGIONARY

DOUGLAS HILL

Alien Citadel

PICCOLO BOOKS

in association with Heinemann

For Lauren and Lisa and Mark
—and Elizabeth too

First published 1984 by William Heinemann Ltd
This Piccolo edition published 1985 by Pan Books Ltd,
Cavaye Place, London SW10 9PG
in association with William Heinemann Ltd

9 8 7 6 5 4 3 2

ISBN 0 330 28563 7

Printed and bound in Great Britain by
Hunt Barnard Printing Ltd, Aylesbury, Bucks.

Contents

PART ONE

The End of the Wasteland

1
Shadow in the Sky

THE DISTANT CLOUDS rose high into the sky, dark smears against its pale springtime blue, stretching out across the land like vast, rolling walls. There were three of them, filling the sky to the north, the east and the west, three sides of an immense rectangle. And the clouds were moving, in a slow but relentless drift towards the south.

They were like the billowing clouds of smoke that accompany the raging advance of a forest fire. But on that land there were no forests to burn. The clouds were formed of dust, rising from the surface of a bleak and arid desert. It was a land of rock and sand and baked earth, broken hills and stony ridges, with only occasional patches of cactus or scrub brush clinging stubbornly to life.

And the clouds of dust were being thrown up from that forbidding terrain by hundreds upon hundreds of strange machines. They were like huge metal eggs, hovering a metre from the ground on swirling cushions of energy beneath their flattened undersides. The downblast from those machines, in their enormous three-sided formation, hurled the dust and sand skyward. And amid those clouds small bat-winged flying creatures, thousands of them, flapped and swooped – their glassy eyes studying every centimetre of the desert, on every side of the advancing machines.

Now and then, the dust-clouds would be streaked with red,

when narrow rays of concentrated heat would leap out from the machines, to blast an outcropping of rock into fragments, or to char a stand of brush into blackened ash.

Those humans who had seen such machines called them whirlsleds. And humans also had a name for the eerie beings who drove the machines. They were beings from another world, who had come, centuries before, with their machines and weapons, to impose their rule upon the Earth. And humans, living in permanent fear of their mysterious and coldly cruel alien masters, had come to call them . . . the Slavers.

The enormous force of Slaver whirlsleds had come on to the desert – known as the Wasteland – early in the spring. Already their slow, methodical, three-sided sweep had passed over more than a third of the desert vastness. And where they had passed, with their blazing heat-weapons, the Wasteland had been truly laid to waste. Hardly a boulder remained intact, hardly a cactus still stood, behind that steady, destructive advance.

Even from a rocky hilltop thirty kilometres away, the towering, menacing clouds of dust were clearly visible. And from that hilltop they were being studied by the calm grey eyes of a young man of about twenty. He was lithe and muscular, with thick straw-coloured hair, and he wore a sleeveless jerkin, trousers and boots all made from soft hide. A heavy knife and a small leather pouch hung from his belt, and around his left wrist was wrapped a broad strip of darker leather.

His name was Finn Ferral, and less than a year before he had been a young village huntsman in the forests far to the east. But since then he had crossed half the continent on a dangerous, relentless search – a search that had at last come to an end among the wild, free people who roamed the Wasteland.

Next to him on that hilltop, also watching the distant, sky-darkening clouds, stood a being who was not human, yet who was Finn's closest friend. His name was Baer, and he was one of a beast-like race called the Bloodkin, descended from humans by means of the cruel science of the alien Slavers. But Baer, more human than other Bloodkin, was a dedicated enemy of his own bestial kind, and their alien masters. No taller than Finn, Baer was immensely broad, his solid hugeness made more obvious because he wore only baggy trousers and heavy boots. Like all Bloodkin, his bulk of muscle was covered by a shaggy pelt of thick hair – and from behind one great shoulder jutted the hilt of a wickedly sharp machete, its sheath strapped to Baer's back.

On the Wasteland during the previous autumn, Finn and Baer had been in the forefront of a terrible battle against a force of Slavers and Bloodkin, led by a malevolent being known as The Claw. The warriors of the Wasteland had won that battle – but now, with the spring, they were facing the deadly aftermath.

For that victory, along with the increasingly bold attacks by the warriors on any lone whirlsleds passing the Wasteland, had brought a response that was perhaps inevitable. The mighty force of Slaver whirlsleds had come on to the Wasteland, to scour and cleanse the entire length and breadth of that region, to rid it of the vermin that infested it.

The vermin that were human beings.

Finn swung his head slightly, sweeping his gaze along the full, frightening lengths of the three distant dust-clouds, east and north and west. "Seems to be more of them all the time," he said calmly. "And more spywings."

"It figures," Baer replied, in a rich bass rumble. "Prob'ly they're comin' from bases all round the Wasteland, not just the Citadel."

Finn nodded. The aliens' base in the mountains to the west, the base known as the Citadel, was the largest Slaver centre in the country. But it was not likely that even the Citadel could provide so many hundreds of whirlsleds for this final, monstrous assault.

"They're not moving any faster," Finn went on. "And they're still keeping their formation, those three straight lines."

"That's Slavers for you," Baer growled. "No imagination – think in straight lines, move in straight lines." He scratched at his vast beard, light-coloured like the rest of his pelt. "Anyways, they don't needta hurry. They know we got only one way to go."

Again Finn nodded, in bleak agreement. Earlier, when the Slaver forces had first begun their advance against the three sides of the Wasteland, parties of warriors had ridden out to see if the lines of whirlsleds could be breached, or bypassed. The warriors were skilled and experienced, able to move almost unseen through areas that would not seem to offer enough cover for a lizard. But they came up against those thousands of sharp-eyed spywings – and the hundreds of whirlsleds, using their lethal heat-weapons against anything that looked like it might be a hiding place for a human.

Not one of those warriors had returned.

So the remaining people of the Wasteland had begun – reluctantly, bitterly, despairingly – a retreat into the southern reaches of the desert, the only direction open to them. And always, small groups ranged forward, as scouts, to make sure that no dangers or ambushes stood in the way of the main body of fleeing people. Finn and Baer were on just such a scouting mission, now, many days after the retreat had begun.

They had paused briefly to rest their horses, and to survey the surrounding terrain from that hilltop. And inevitably, they had also looked back at the towering barrier of the dust clouds.

Finn's vision rivalled that of a hunting hawk – just as in many other ways he was as much a wild creature as a man. But even his eyes could not discern the whirlsleds themselves, hidden within the distant clouds. Yet the clouds alone were menacing enough, in their immense breadth. At that distance they seemed to have nearly joined together at the ends, looking less like three separate sides of a rectangle, more like a gigantic, sweeping crescent or arc. It made Finn suddenly think of the blade of a sickle – a vast and deadly curve of metal, slicing slowly across the Wasteland towards a final harvest of death.

Despite the sun's heat, he shivered slightly at that mental image. Then he firmly turned his back on the monstrous walls of dust, and looked southwards.

As Baer said, it was the only way that the Wasteland people could go. And the people had come to believe that they were being purposefully *driven* in that direction – like beasts being herded into a trap. For lying to the south was another desert region, far more terrible even than the harsh and barren Wasteland. It was a place created by ancient evil, a place of nightmare, unnatural terror, invisible and ever-present death. An area called the Firesands.

When the Wasteland people were driven at last, by the Slavers' merciless advance, to the edge of that ghastly region, they knew that they would face the cruellest of choices. Whether to turn and try to fight the whirlsleds – and be slaughtered by the aliens' superior weapons – or whether to continue their retreat, into the fearsome depths of the Firesands. One choice would bring certain, quick death; the other way would bring very probable, slow and terrible death.

Either way, the people knew, they were facing the end of their free, brave life on the Wasteland.

Again Finn shivered, as he thought those dire thoughts. But then he shook himself, and pointed with a steady hand to a group of low hills, a few kilometres south from where he and Baer stood.

"There's supposed to be a waterhole in there," he told Baer. "Let's have a look at it while we're here."

"Suits me," Baer rumbled. He shook the leather water-bottle tied to his belt. "We could do with a refill."

They moved away down the hillside, towards their horses –

sturdy desert mustangs, the sturdiest being the one that had to carry Baer's great weight. Finn seemed scarcely to look at the ground, yet he moved by instinct in a total silence – seeming to drift forward without rattling a pebble, as a wolf or a cougar might have silently padded down from that hilltop. And even Baer, despite his bulk and heavy boots, had been with Finn long enough to have acquired some of those wilderness skills, so that he too crossed that stretch of rough terrain in near-silence.

They rode away, not hurrying, and always – again by instinct and habit – keeping a wary watch on every dip and fold in the land, every boulder and outcrop. And they were still moving just as watchfully, some while later, when they reached a dusty slope that would bring them, on the far side, to the water-hole.

There they dismounted, leading their horses. At the top of the slope, they crouched and peered down. The water-hole lay about a quarter of a kilometre away, a stretch of green and brown foliage in a shallow basin of land. Like many of the scattered oases in that grim desert, it was dotted with shrubs and low trees that looked unnatural in their distorted, twisted shapes. But Finn was used to such sights on the Wasteland. His keen eyes were making sure that there were no other shapes, even more unnatural and alien, among the foliage.

But then his attention was caught by a movement, on the westward side of the water-hole. It was a shadow, drifting rapidly along the ground, as if cast by a wind-driven cloud, or by a soaring buzzard. Finn's head jerked up – and he froze, eyes wide. Next to him, also looking up, Baer grunted as if he had been struck.

The sky was cloudless, and there were no buzzards. The shadow was being cast by a flying object. A machine.

It was made of darkly shiny metal, bristling with rods and tubes and strange extensions. And it was shaped vaguely like an oval, but distorted enough to betray its alien origin.

The shadow grew larger as the alien machine descended, with a growling throb of powerful engines. But Finn was sure that whatever was inside the machine had not seen himself or Baer, crouched on that slope. The machine was dropping down towards the water-hole.

Then it seemed to pause, and hover. One of the jutting metal tubes swivelled, pointing downwards. From the tip of that rod, a stripe of crimson, lurid and intense, lanced out and down with a sizzling hiss.

And the undergrowth around the water-hole, where the crimson ray struck, exploded into bright flame.

2
Aliens

AS THE OASIS blazed, the weird flying machine continued its descent, engines grumbling. And Finn, even more wide-eyed with astonishment, turned to Baer.

"Is that thing one of the Slaver spaceships?" he asked, in a low voice.

"Could be," Baer muttered. "But I never saw it before."

Finn frowned. Baer had been born and raised in the aliens' mountain Citadel, before he had finally broken away from the Slavers and his own brutal kind. There was little he did not know about his former masters.

"There were some whatyacallem – spaceships," Baer went on. "Came an' went every once in a while. But they were lots bigger'n this one. Bigger'n the Citadel itself."

Finn shook his head, not sure he wanted to know such a disturbing fact, and turned back to watch the strange ship. It was settling to the ground, near the oasis – where the flames were dying, leaving nothing but blackened skeletons of brush, and smouldering ash.

As it touched down, a seam on one side of the ship began slowly to open, like a wound, to form a high narrow doorway. And through that opening stalked the weirdly shaped forms of four Slavers.

They were tall, with long spindly arms and legs that went oddly with their solid, bulging torsos – which, Finn knew, were protected by a hard covering like an insect's shell, a nearly invulnerable armour. On skinny necks, their heads displayed only a slash of mouth and rectangular eyes that, normally, glowed a luminous yellow. And in their three-clawed hands they held slim metal tubes – smaller versions of the weapon, called a heatlance, that the ship had fired at the oasis.

The four aliens marched to the edge of the charred undergrowth and bent, as if examining something. Finn saw that it was the remains of some creature, caught in the fire. Clearly it had been one of the weird Wasteland mutations – a tiny, malformed body, and far too many long spidery legs.

But it looked almost normal compared to the thing that emerged next from the spaceship.

Finn's heart seemed almost to stop, as he stared. It was chillingly monstrous – about four metres tall, he guessed, and enormously bulky. Yet it was vaguely human in shape, with arms and legs and head in the right places. And then, through his amazement, Finn realized that the bulk might not really be a part of the monster. It seemed to be wearing a covering of some kind, like a suit of shiny, flexible metal. Finn could clearly see seams and fastenings on the outside of the suit.

The monster lumbered slowly towards the Slavers, and stooped to look at the dead beast. And Finn turned again to Baer.

"Don't look at me," Baer said hoarsely. He seemed as astounded as Finn. "I never saw anythin' like that before, anywhere."

The four Slavers, directed by the towering monster, picked up the dead creature and stalked back towards the ship. The monster gazed around for a moment, before following. Shortly, with a low thunder of engines, the ship lifted off, drifting slowly away towards the south.

Finn watched it fixedly, as it receded into the distance. It was flying low – and before it vanished even from his sight, he saw it dip down lower, as if settling towards another landing, many kilometres into the southern wastes.

"I figure," Baer rumbled, "we're really done for, now."

Finn had been thinking the same thing. The moving walls of whirlsleds had been bad enough – leaving the Wasteland people only a remote hope of temporary survival in the lethal depths of the Firesands. But now it seemed they had no hope at all. Not if the Slavers were bringing their spaceships, as well, into action.

That had been the constant nightmare of Earth's human survivors – that a time would come when the aliens would no longer be willing to put up with the existence of even a remnant of humanity. The Slavers had tried to exterminate humans once before, using their spaceships, soon after they arrived. Now it seemed that the ships were to be used again. And not even the Wasteland warriors would find a place to hide from them.

Finn's mouth twisted in a grimace that was not quite a smile. "I guess we made trouble for them once too often," he said.

"Seems so," Baer agreed, his own grin just as mirthless. "But it was a risk we always knew we were runnin'."

Finn nodded bleakly, then rose and shook himself. "Let's go see what that fire did to the water-hole."

They mounted up, and rode warily down towards the blackened oasis. But before they reached its edge, Finn's hearing picked up the distant drumming of horses' hooves. Another group of scouts, he knew – for no one but the warriors rode horses on the Wasteland.

Soon the mounted figures came into sight, and Finn saw that there were three of them. One was a tall, bare-chested young man with copper-brown skin and a stripe of white paint across his face. He wore leggings and high boots of soft hide, and carried a long slim spear. The other two were women – a girl of about sixteen, fair-haired and shapely, and a broad-shouldered woman with a tangled mane of red hair. Both wore short tunics also of soft hide, and had bows and arrows slung at their backs.

"Jena, Rainshadow and Marakela," Finn told Baer, who was squinting at the distant figures.

Rainshadow was one of the leaders of the wild desert Indians who made up the largest part of the Wasteland population. Marakela led a band of equally wild and fierce women warriors. And Jena was Finn's foster sister – whom he had been seeking, in his grim quest across the continent, and whom he had found, safe, among the Wasteland warriors, a fully fledged warrior herself.

As they drew near, the three newcomers were staring at the devastated oasis. "Who started the fire?" Marakela called.

But when Finn had bluntly told them what it was that had destroyed the water-hole, even Rainshadow turned pale under the coppery sheen of his skin.

"Then it is the end of us, without doubt," the young Indian said. His voice was flat, almost fatalistic.

"Not just yet," Baer growled. "We can still slice a few Slaver necks 'fore they finish us."

Rainshadow shook his head. "Not when they are in whirlsleds, or in machines in the sky."

Finn looked at Jena, a sadness in his eyes. "It almost makes me glad that Josh didn't make it," he said quietly.

Josh was Finn's foster father, and Jena's real father, Joshua Ferral. The previous year, Finn and Baer had rescued Josh and some other humans from a small Slaver base in the east. Josh and his group had then decided to follow Finn and Baer westward, towards the Wasteland. They had intended to move more slowly than Finn and Baer, on that danger-filled journey. Even so, many months had passed – and neither Josh nor any of his companions had reached the western deserts.

Jena's eyes had filled with tears, but there was as much anger as grief in her voice. "What's worst of all," she said, "is not *knowing* what happened to him." She stared round at the burnt-out oasis, then up at the empty sky. "And now I guess we'll never know."

Marakela snorted. "You're all talkin' like we're gonna be dead by sun-down! So maybe we got spaceships after us now, too. But we don't just lie down an' say, okay, come an' kill us!"

Baer laughed. "Atta girl! Why don't you go after that spaceship, an' beat up on it all by yourself?"

The others laughed as well, though the bleakness did not leave their eyes. But Finn did not join in the laughter. He was looking away, as if he had not heard Baer – staring thoughtfully across the desert, southwards.

Baer, still grinning, did not notice. "Anyways, I'd as soon not die of *thirst*." He jerked a broad thumb towards the ruin of the oasis. "Let's go see what the fire did to the water, in there."

The five of them dismounted, and moved carefully in among the blackened stumps and ashes. And they were relieved to find, at the centre, that the small pool of water, fed by an underground spring, was still intact.

They brushed aside the layer of ash that had settled on the pool's surface. Then each of them stooped to drink, and to refill their water bottles. Each of them but Finn.

When the others turned to look curiously at him, they saw that he was still staring blankly into the distance. And the others glanced at one another, with expressions that were slightly worried.

They all knew him very well. And they had all seen that look on his face before, during the past months of danger and bloodshed.

"Finn," Baer rumbled, "what's goin' on in that head of yours?"

Finn started slightly, as if coming awake. "I was just thinking," he said lamely.

"We noticed," Jena said. "And you have that look – like you have when you're dreaming up some wild idea."

Finn smiled faintly. "I was thinking about what Baer said to Marakela. About following the spaceship."

Marakela's laughter boomed. "You may be better'n any of us in the wilds, Finn, but even you can't track a flyin' machine!"

"Even flying machines come down to land sometimes," Finn

told her. "And that one looked like it was landing. Over that way." He pointed southwards. "So – I was thinking I might ride south awhile."

They all looked at him, seeing the steady eyes, the firm set of his jaw. And they recalled other times when he had looked like that. When he had gone alone into a Slaver base to find Joshua Ferral, and free him. When he had gone alone to rescue Baer, and had single-handedly destroyed nearly half of the force that The Claw had led into the Wasteland.

"Finn," Rainshadow said, with the tone of one who knows his argument will not be listened to, "the edge of the Firesands is less than a day's ride from here."

Finn shrugged. "I know. Maybe I won't need to go that far. Maybe the ship has come down somewhere nearer. Maybe it has flown away again. But I won't *know*, unless I ride south."

"There you go again," Baer grumbled. "You been doin' that ever since we met. So I'll say it again. *You're* not ridin' south, boy. *We* are."

"We all are," Jena said firmly.

Finn looked doubtful, but before he could protest Marakela laughed again. "C'mon, young Finn, stop tryin' t' fight this war all by y'rself. We're comin' with y'. Spaceships, big monsters in metal suits – I wouldn't miss it fer anythin'."

"A time may come when you wish you had," Rainshadow said gravely.

Jena looked at him, eyebrows raised. "That doesn't sound like you."

The young Indian grunted. "Perhaps not. But I have a feeling – a coldness, like a warning. I do not think we should try to follow that spaceship." He sighed and shook his head. "But since I know that Finn will go anyway, I agree that we should ride with him, and keep him out of trouble."

"An' if we do find that ship on the ground somewhere," Baer rumbled, "maybe the five of us can think of somethin' to do to it."

3

Discovery

AFTER WATERING THEIR horses, the five set off towards the south. As always, they kept a careful watch on their surroundings – but the rugged land and sun-filled sky seemed empty of any threat. So they rode at a steady pace, moving in almost a straight line towards the spot where Finn had seen the alien spaceship dip down towards the ground.

They rode in silence, each wrapped in thought. At first Finn was thinking about little more than the spaceship, and the weirdly tall, metal-suited being that had emerged from it. But those thoughts led to others – including disturbing thoughts about the Firesands, and how they had come into existence, back in the ancient days that Finn's people called the Forgotten Time . . .

It was a time, Finn knew, when there were countless humans on the Earth. And when those humans made huge cities of metal and stone, and filled them with fantastic machines, and greedily robbed the Earth of its natural riches in order to maintain their artificial lives.

And they were greedy for power as well as wealth. They created terrible weapons – and, because men who have weapons will always use them, a time came when a hideous war had virtually set the world on fire.

Nothing of human civilization survived that war, and very little of humanity itself. The survivors skulked and mourned among the rubble of the world, ablaze with the lethal fire called 'radioactivity'. Pockets of that invisible death still remained, centuries later, in Finn's time, as in the Firesands.

But back in the Forgotten Time, many of the surviving humans were tough and brave enough to try to rebuild their world, over the following century or two, or three. Until they ran out of time.

That had happened with crushing suddenness, on a day when the skies over Earth were filled with gigantic, oddly-shaped flying machines. Machines that carried the spindly-limbed, yellow-eyed aliens who from then on were the Earth's new masters.

No one knew where they came from, or why. There was never any communication between the people of Earth and the invaders. The aliens ignored the humans, or coldly killed any who got in the way. And when the humans gathered courage and weapons, and rose up against the invaders, the huge alien ships lifted again into the sky, with their powerful heat-weapons. And once again the Earth was set aflame.

Everything that had been rebuilt, even the ruins of the old civilization, was wiped out in that terrible onslaught. And the human survivors of that new horror – now no more than a few thousand of them – fled into the wilderness that had spread itself over so much of the ravaged land.

There they sank into empty, miserable lives in crude villages scattered through the wilds, over which the shadow of terror always lay. For the aliens did not leave them alone.

They sent out their batlike spywings, to watch for more signs of resistance, or for attempts to rebuild any of the old civilization. If the spywings saw signs of such activity, whirlsleds would come, heatlances would blaze, and people would die. But sometimes the whirlsleds came to a village for another reason – to take some humans away into the unknown nightmare of captivity. Out of those times of terror and loss, humans had come to give their alien masters a name – the Slavers.

That way of life, if it could be called life, had been going on for two or more centuries before the day when Slavers came to the forest village where Finn Ferral had grown up. And when they left, they took with them the only family Finn had ever known – Joshua Ferral, and Jena.

Most humans would have simply suffered the grief and pain, as if the Slavers were a kind of natural calamity, like disease. But Finn was different. No one knew where he had come from, and that made him different. So did his uncanny, natural affinity for the wilderness. And he was set further apart from other humans when he did what no other would have dared – when he set off alone on his determined, relentless quest.

That quest led to many things – especially to times of violence and danger. It led to his friendship with Baer. And it led eventually to the Slaver base from which he and Baer had freed the slaves who included Josh Ferral.

But in that alien base, as well, Finn had learned the shattering truth about his own origin.

Finn had been just a toddler when Josh had found him, alone and unafraid, in the depths of the forest. And Josh never solved the mystery of where Finn had come from – nor if there was any meaning in the odd pattern of raised dark dots on the boy's upper left arm. But years later, in that Slaver base, Finn learned the terrible answer to those mysteries.

Baer had told him that sometimes the Slavers forced young men and women slaves to mate – and then, long before the babies from those unions were born, the aliens performed strange operations on them in eerie laboratories. But the only babies born *alive* after those operations had always been the savage, beast-like Bloodkin. And Finn had seen those ugly facts for himself, inside the Slaver base, when he found human women who had given birth to Bloodkin babies. He had also found the corpses of normal human babies which, as was always the case, had not survived the Slavers' alterations.

But then he learned the mind-shattering truth. Each of those small normal bodies had had, on the upper left arm, a pattern of raised dark dots.

So at least *one* normal human infant had been created, and born alive, in a Slaver laboratory. And that infant was himself, Finn Ferral.

Baer had helped Finn to recover from that shock by explaining the Slavers' purposes. The aliens were trying to breed new humans, erasing their intelligence, making them more like docile animals. But with Finn, the experiment had gone wrong. The Slavers had not erased his humanity. Instead, they had accidentally *added* something to it – the natural, inborn abilities and instincts of a wild creature.

From that Slaver base Finn and Baer had headed westward, leaving old Josh and the other slaves – led by a scar-faced man named Gratton – to make their own slower way in the same direction. Finn's goal was the enormous Citadel of the Slavers, in the far western mountains, where he believed Jena may have been taken. But then they had found Jena on the Wasteland, among the warriors, having been rescued from a Slaver whirlsled by Marakela and her fearless women. So Finn's long quest was over.

But the danger was not. The Slavers had also learned that he existed, as the only normal survivor of their ghastly experiments. So the aliens sent their deadly servant, The Claw, in pursuit of Finn.

The Claw had been defeated – but now the Wasteland was paying the price. As Finn had said, the warriors had troubled the Slavers once too often. The monstrous three-sided force of whirlsleds had come to scour the desert. And it now seemed that with them, to make sure of that final extermination, had come an even more terrible force – the Slaver spaceships.

* * *

But as Finn mulled over these memories and forebodings, he was feeling neither fearful nor despairing. True to his nature, the strongest feelings within him during that silent ride were a stubborn refusal to admit defeat, and a wild creature's undying curiosity.

He wanted to see that spaceship again, despite the Slavers and the giant, metal-suited monster. And, like Baer, he wanted to see if there might be some way to disable the ship – to strike at least that blow against the aliens' superior might.

After a ride of some hours, he and his companions drew near to the place where Finn had seen the ship dip downwards. They dismounted, and crept unseen to peer over the edge of a low, steep cliff. And a fierce excitement swept through Finn.

The strange craft *had* landed. It rested in the centre of a wide, flat expanse of dry earth. The tall doorway in its side stood open, a rectangle of blackness. It was silent, and still, like some darkened alien tomb.

But then the five heads turned at once, as they all glimpsed the distant movement.

It was the four Slavers from the ship, marching stiffly along some distance away. They seemed to be making their way towards a low dip in the land, partly clogged with dry, twisted thorn bushes.

"Y'know," Baer said casually, "we could circle around outa sight, an' jump those critturs."

"Just what I was thinkin'," Marakela said with a fierce grin.

Jena and Rainshadow readily agreed – but Finn remained still. "Go ahead," he told them. "I'll stay here and watch the ship."

The others paused, peering at him. "You'll really stay *here*?" Jena asked, voicing the thought of all of them.

Finn gazed at her innocently. "Where else would I go?"

Jena frowned dubiously – but Marakela was growing impatient. So finally she turned away, to join the others as they moved in silent pursuit of the aliens.

And Finn turned back to look at the ship. With the Slavers out of the way, he thought, was the tall monster alone in there? Or had it gone exploring on its own, elsewhere in the desert? So he waited, and watched, and wondered . . .

The other four covered the distance swiftly. Yet it would have taken an eagle eye to have spotted them, as they ghosted across that broken, rocky landscape. And within a few moments they were moving, silent as puffs of dust, along the fringes of the patch of thorn bush.

The four Slavers were still advancing – with heatlances in their hands, but without seeming very alert or wary. Clearly they believed themselves to be alone in the midst of a desolate desert. Then they reached the thorn bushes, and learned otherwise.

One of the aliens suddenly fell, a feathered arrow jutting from one eye. In the same instant a second alien fell, a long slender spear driving into the centre of its face.

The eyes of the other two changed colour, darkening to a cold purplish-blue. But they had barely begun to raise their heat-lances when Baer and Marakela surged out of the brush on either side. Baer's machete swung in a glittering arc, and a third alien fell, headless, to the ground. And Marakela did not even bother with a weapon, but merely seized the scrawny neck of the fourth Slaver in her powerful hands, and twisted. There was a small crunch, and the last alien corpse crumpled at her feet.

"That was almost too easy," she said, gazing down with some satisfaction.

The others grinned, and Jena and Rainshadow stepped forward to reclaim their arrow and spear. But then they froze, as if they had turned to stone.

Something in the depths of the brush had, very faintly, moaned.

The four moved silently forward, both Jena and Marakela drawing sharp knives from their belts. Not a twig rustled as they crept deeper into the patch of brush. And then they came to a small, clear area near the centre of the patch. Again they froze – not with wariness, but with sheer astonishment.

There were two humans in that area. Perhaps they were what the four Slavers had been seeking. Both were ragged and dusty, and one of them – a big man with a ridged scar across his face – lay unconscious, with a gruesome, gaping wound in his leg.

The other man was smaller, slightly stooped, with grey hair and a grizzled beard, yet lean and leathery and wiry. He seemed weary and tense – but he staggered to his feet, staring with amazement at the four people who had suddenly appeared out of the brush. And his blue eyes were gleaming, and his lined face was crinkling with an enormous smile.

"Well, lookit here," Baer said softly.

And then, with a small muffled cry, Jena sprung forward – and threw her arms around her father, Joshua Ferral.

4
Within the Spaceship

"SO HE FOUND YOU," Josh said to his daughter.

Those were nearly the first coherent words he had spoken. It had taken several moments for both Josh and Jena to emerge from the tidal wave of emotion that had swept over them, the staggering joy that each of them had felt at their unexpected reunion. And during that time the others had stood and grinned, sharing some of that emotion, and there was even a hint of dampness in the twinkling eyes beneath Baer's shaggy brows.

Then, for several more minutes, there was a torrent of talk. Jena had introduced Rainshadow and Marakela, and had briefly told her father about life on the Wasteland. And the old man had listened and nodded, never taking his eyes from Jena's shining face.

"Yes, he found me," Jena said, laughing. "And now we've found you. And . . ." Suddenly her face crumpled, as she remembered what was happening on the rest of the Wasteland, beyond that joyful patch of brush. "And it's all happened too *late*!" she burst out.

Josh frowned anxiously. "What's too late?"

"Uh . . ." Baer broke in, not wanting to see Josh hurled into despair so soon after joy. "It's nothin', Josh. Anyways, it's time *you* did some talkin'. What's wrong with Gratton? An' where're the rest of the folks?"

Josh turned to Baer, the smile fading from his face. The two of them had become good friends in the days after Josh had been freed from the Slaver base, in the east. So Baer could read the grim answer to his last question in the sudden bleakness of the old man's eyes.

"Gone," Josh said hollowly. "Dead – all of 'em. 'Cept us two."

He told the terrible story in a low, flat voice. The group of ex-slaves had started out well – led by big Gratton, the scar-faced man, and fed by the skills of Josh who had himself been a huntsman all his life. But many of the group had been young women who had suffered in the Slavers' cruel experiments. Some were carrying their infants – small, furry, Bloodkin babies – and others were pregnant. And the gruelling days of travel soon took their toll.

"A coupla girls died givin' birth," Josh said bleakly. "Nothin' we c'd do for 'em. Then some more died from some kinda disease, men as well as women. An' we lost a few more, drowned, when we hadta cross a big river."

Finally there had been only seven of the group left, as they crossed the vast central plains. And there they had been caught in an unusually fierce prairie winter. Arctic winds and savage blizzards had cut the small party down further. Until at last only Josh and Gratton remained, stumbling on through sheer grit and will-power.

Josh's voice drifted into silence, stilled by those grim memories. As he had been speaking, Rainshadow had gone over to crouch by Gratton's unconscious form.

"His wound is poisoned," the young Indian said. "It must be treated soon."

"I know," Josh said wearily. "He cut his leg on some rocks, a few days ago. I been helpin' him – but t'day he passed out, an' I can't carry him. I figured he was finished . . . 'cause I was sure by then that Baer was right, back east, when he said there weren't people on the Wasteland."

Baer grinned crookedly, remembering how sure he had been of that fact. "Sometimes seems there's more folks here than in all the rest of the country."

"An' lots of'em know about fixin' wounds," Marakela put in. "So let's hoist up y'r big friend, go get Finn, an' get outa here."

"I'd sure like that," Josh said fervently. "Can't hardly believe I'm gonna have my family t'gether again." He swung an arm around Jena and hugged her.

"C'mon, then," Baer said. He lumbered over to Gratton, and scooped up the heavy, limp body as if it were a sack of feathers. "Me, I can hardly wait to see the look on Finn's face when he sees the surprise we're bringin' with us!"

But by then, Finn was working on a surprise of his own.

After his friends had left, he had seen the four Slavers disappear into the fringes of the pocket of thorn bushes. And he had not seen them come out again. Knowing his friends as he did, he had smiled a small savage smile.

But most of the time he had been studying the silent spaceship, with its temptingly open door. He had shifted position twice, drifting invisibly over the rough ground, for a better view. But not even his hawk eyes could penetrate the darkness of that doorway – made even darker by the dazzle of the sun reflecting from the metal of the ship's side.

At the same time Finn had listened intently – and had heard only dust stirred by a light desert breeze, and the distant scuttle of some tiny creature. He had sniffed the air – and though his sense of smell was as acute as a wolf's, he had scented only hot sand and the faint odour of alien metal.

So he grew dissatisfied, and restless. He had wanted to see the towering alien monster more closely. But it was not likely that the being was inside the ship. For if it was, then surely it would be moving around – and Finn's uncanny hearing would have detected the sounds. But if it was *not* in the ship, if it had wandered off into the desert for reasons of its own, then the ship was probably empty. And vulnerable.

The longer that Finn sat there, the more convinced he became that the ship was unoccupied. But of course, that was what he wanted to believe. Because it meant that he could do what his restlessness and his curiosity were urging him to do.

Tense and wary, he rose from his hiding place and began to make his way towards the ship.

He stayed well out of any line of sight from the dark doorway. He moved in a catlike crouch, or sometimes slid forward flat on his belly. He took advantage of every rock, every bump or dip in the land. And a man standing even twenty metres away would probably not have seen even a flicker of movement, as Finn drew near to his goal.

Finally he was there, crouched low, pressed against the hot metal of the ship's hull near the open doorway. Again he stared around, and listened, and sniffed.

Nothing. No sound of movement from the dark interior. And only a left-over trace of the faintly sour smell of Slavers – and another, even fainter, slightly sickly odour that he could not recognize.

There was no question about it, he assured himself. The ship was deserted.

He edged forward slowly. He resembled a wild animal that is strongly tempted by a desirable morsel of food, while instinctively fearing that it might be bait for a trap. The temptation pulls it forward, the fear holds it back. Yet, tragically often, the temptation wins. The creature moves forward, hesitantly, one quivering step at a time, but still forward.

So Finn moved, as temptation drew him. And still he heard no sound, sensed no danger, as he stepped watchfully through the doorway, into the alien ship.

As his eyes quickly adjusted to the dimness, he stared around. All of his uncanny senses were at their highest pitch, and every nerve was vibrating with tension. But nothing happened – no movement, no sound, no sign of a living thing anywhere within that interior. So in a moment or two he relaxed slightly, and began to explore.

At one end of the area that he found himself in, he saw two cushioned objects that, he slowly realized, were an odd combination of seat and bed. They were angled, so that anyone seated in them would be half-reclining. And they were huge – more than four metres long. So they had to be designed for beings like the giant, metal-suited monster.

In front of the seats he saw a sweep of strange machinery, dominated by large screens that glowed a dim green. In among them were rows of switches and buttons and levers, many more small dim lights, and a host of other objects that meant nothing to Finn. And there were banks of more weird alien machinery on either side of the seats, reaching up almost to the slightly curved roof.

The idea came to Finn that he might press some of those switches and buttons, pull some of the levers. Perhaps just as he was about to leave the ship – so that he could dive out through the door if it began to close. In that way he might succeed in doing some kind of damage to the ship, perhaps even disabling it.

But first, he thought, there was more to see. At the other end of the area, which was half as long as the ship, stood a blank metal wall, which held another tall narrow door. That door was closed – but was still another temptation.

Stealthy as a shadow, Finn crept towards that doorway.

Again he paused, to listen and sniff. He heard not the ghost of a movement. And again he smelled only the trace of the four Slavers' presence, and that odd sickly odour – slightly stronger now. He had no idea what it was, but then he had no idea what most of the things were, around him, inside that alien vessel. So he ignored it, and reached out towards the small, nearly square touch-panel that would open the door.

The rectangle of metal slid quietly aside. As tensely and

hesitantly as before, and just as determinedly, Finn slid through the doorway.

The second area where he found himself was even more shadowy, but Finn could see well enough. He saw that there were tall, box-shaped containers standing here and there around him, and other containers lying flat. Inside the containers he could see the dim outlines of weird shapes – and recognized them as some of the mutant creatures from the southern stretches of the Wasteland. So, he began to understand, the metal-suited monster was *collecting* the creatures, for some reason, and storing them in strange transparent containers.

The sickly odour seemed even stronger, but still it told Finn nothing. He took a wary step forward, into the area, and then another. The movements were absolutely soundless. Not even his breathing made a quiver of sound in the air. Yet, despite all his tension and instinctive caution, he was still convinced that he was the only living thing, at that moment, inside the spaceship.

Because of that certainty, he relaxed a little. He had no idea that as he entered that darkened second area, he was clearly visible, framed against the dim glow of the screens and the machinery at the other end of the ship.

The sudden sound beside him was very faint, like a soft gargling cough, as if someone was trying to clear his throat without being heard. But the total unexpectedness of it froze Finn where he stood – his neck-hairs lifting, his skin prickling with a wash of icy fear.

He had just begun to turn when he heard the second sound. A faint clink, like metal brushing against metal.

His hand flashed to the hilt of the heavy knife at his belt, as he completed the turn. And another icy chill swept over him as he saw the shadowy form rise up before him. It was rising from something that he had thought, at a glance, was another of the large containers – but that was in fact some kind of couch, with raised sides. A very long couch.

The shadowy form loomed towards him, huge and towering. As Finn drew his knife, he saw the thing swinging something through the air towards him. Something like a huge, elongated arm, but sheathed in heavy metal.

He tried to dodge, to leap away, and to use his knife, all at once. He only partly succeeded in doing any of those things.

The knife glanced harmlessly off shiny metal. Then the enormous arm smashed against the side of his head in an agonizing inner explosion of bright light – which faded, and dwindled, and vanished, as he toppled down into darkness.

PART TWO

Slave of the Citadel

5
Steelfinder

HE CAME AWAKE as a wild animal does, every sense instantly alert, every muscle poised for swift movement. And in that first instant of waking, Finn was aware of several different sensations at once.

First was pain – a throbbing ache within his skull, and two more localized points, on either side of his head. There were also lesser areas of pain that burned and stung all down the left side of his body.

Also, he had known at the moment of waking that he was lying on a hard, bare, metal floor. When his eyes opened, he saw that he was in a large room, with metal walls that gave off their own dim glow of illumination. And his nose had told him even before his eyes that he was not alone in that room.

He looked swiftly around, braced against the jolt of misery that he knew would hit him if he saw Jena or the others. But then he sagged with relief. There were many other humans scattered around the floor, curled up in uncomfortable sleeping positions. But they were strangers. And all of them seemed to be keeping their distance from Finn, huddling near the wall at the far end of the chamber. They were ragged and filthy, and the room stank – not only of unwashed human bodies, but with the acid reek of human fear. And through that odour Finn's sensitive nostrils detected the thick, rank scent of Bloodkin.

But he did not need that smell to tell him where he was. He

had seen a chamber like this before – when he had freed Josh and the others from the Slaver base in the east. It was the solidly locked room where the aliens put their human slaves at night. And because he had been taken from the Wasteland, this chamber could be in only one Slaver base. The Citadel.

The awareness brought with it, in that instant of waking, a surge of fear and rage and despair. For a moment he was no longer a young man, but a wild beast – trapped, caged, frantic and panicky in its terror. He pushed himself up from the floor, lips twisted into a snarl, the whites of his eyes glinting with near-hysteria. He might then have flung himself mindlessly at the metal walls, as a caged beast might hopelessly attack the unyielding bars that surround it.

But the sudden movement brought a new eruption of pain, a stabbing fire in his head. A wave of dizziness poured over him, and he swayed. Then he caught himself, gritting his teeth, waiting till the dizziness passed and the pain dwindled slightly. And in that time he fought and overcame the hysteria, fought to regain his humanity, his reason and self-awareness. At last, slowly, he reached up to touch his head with careful fingertips.

On the right side of his head he found a large swelling, and a cut in his scalp from which blood had matted his hair. But it was no longer bleeding, and as far as he could tell – with relief – there was none of the sponginess that would suggest a crushed or fractured skull.

On the left side of his head he felt another, smaller swelling, and a deeper cut, which seemed to have bled profusely. But there too the bleeding had stopped, and no serious damage had been done.

He paused, thoughtfully. He remembered being attacked in the alien ship – by the huge, metal-suited monster that must have been lying silently on its couch, perhaps asleep, all the time. The monster had clubbed him, with its metal-clad arm – but on the right side of the head.

So, he guessed, he had fallen and struck the *left* side of his head on some other object – probably one of the large containers. That would also explain the stinging hurts he felt on his left side.

He turned his head carefully to examine himself. And then, astonishingly, he smiled, with a savage amusement.

During Finn's raid on the Slaver base in the east, the aliens had learned of his existence – as the only normal human survivor of their evil experiments. Ever since then, they had urgently wanted to capture him, to find out *why* he had survived. So it was odd that when they actually *had* captured him, they would simply dump him in with the rest of the slaves and ignore him.

But in that glance down at the left side of his body, he had seen why he was being ignored.

His fall, in the spaceship, against some sharp and solid edge, had damaged more than the left side of his head. His left shoulder and upper arm were also bruised, with several small cuts and grazes. They too had bled, and the blood had dried.

And the dried blood was masking the marks that identified his origin – the strange pattern of raised dark dots on his upper left arm.

So to the Slavers and their Bloodkin, he was just another human captive. And because slaves were treated appallingly in an alien base, there was no chance that he would ever need to wash away the dried blood. He had no idea what the Slavers would have done with him, had they known who he was. But he was deeply thankful for the good luck that meant he would not have to find out.

He continued to take stock of himself and his surroundings. He was still wearing his normal clothes, though of course without his knife or belt pouch, or the sling that was usually wrapped round his left wrist. But at least the rest of his body seemed uninjured – and even the pounding headache was beginning to fade slightly. Aside from that, his only discomfort was a raging thirst, and the hardness of the metal floor.

He glanced again around the chamber. The other people numbered only about two dozen, though the chamber seemed large enough to hold three times that many. There were men of various ages, and a number of older women – those who were past child-bearing age, Finn thought grimly. He knew that young women were kept apart, to be used in the cruel alien experiments.

Since he knew none of the sleeping people, Finn realized that they must all have come from other parts of the country, not from the Wasteland. But as he looked around, a woman over by the far wall stirred and turned restlessly in her sleep. And Finn, only then seeing her face clearly, saw with a start that she, at least, he did know – because she was a Wasteland warrior.

She had short, straight black hair, streaked with grey, and her copper-brown skin was drawn tight over the prominent bones of her face. She wore a short tunic, like Marakela and Jena, but also the leggings and knee-high boots of the desert Indian. Her name was Steelfinder, since she was renowned for having discovered a deposit of the ancient metal – strange machines that had survived intact from the Forgotten Times – which the warriors used to forge their weapons.

As if aware in her sleep of Finn's gaze, the woman suddenly opened her eyes. Seeing Finn sitting up, she smiled faintly, rose and came over to him.

"Finn." She might have been greeting him casually as they passed one another in a Wasteland camp. "How do you feel?"

"My head hurts," Finn replied, "but nothing's broken, as far as I can tell."

She raised three fingers. "How many fingers?"

Finn blinked, puzzled, and told her.

"Good." She seemed pleased. "At worst, only a small concussion. You will be fine."

Finn grimaced. "I'd be better if I had some water."

Steelfinder's faint smile appeared again. "The Bloodkin give us food and water only when they bring us in here at night. It is filthy, but it goes quickly. Still, I knew you would need something when you woke."

She reached into her tunic, and brought out a ragged scrap of cloth – soaking wet. It was dirty, and the water that had soaked it had been foul. But Finn took it gratefully, squeezing the liquid into his mouth, feeling the grinding headache fade away a little more.

Then Steelfinder took the cloth and began to dab, gently but painfully, at the matted blood on Finn's head. "You have a hard skull," she said matter-of-factly.

"Just as well," Finn muttered. Then he jerked away, as Steelfinder was about to turn her attention to his left arm. "Don't worry about that," he said quickly. "It's just grazed."

She raised her eyebrows, but said nothing. And Finn sought a new subject. "Were any other slaves brought in with me?" he asked.

Steelfinder shook her head. "We were all at work, outside, when the flying machine landed. Slavers went in and brought you out. No one else."

Finn was glad to have that proof that none of his friends had been captured – since it was possible that Baer, and especially Jena, would not have been put with the other slaves if they had been taken. But then, he thought, they might have found me gone and tried to attack the ship. Maybe they had all been killed. There was no way for him to know. Perhaps, he thought bitterly, he would never know.

He stared around the room again. There was a wide metal door at one end, but it would be solidly fastened. And on the outside, he knew, there would be a strange screen or barrier of energy – like the sparkling fire that drove the hovering whirlsleds. That door could never be opened from inside the slave chamber.

Steelfinder was watching him, with her faint smile. "You are thinking about escape. But I have been here for weeks, Finn. And though I know what things you have done, I can tell you that even you could never escape from here."

Finn looked at her emptily. "This *is* the Citadel?"

She nodded, and he went on. "Did you see . . . anything else come out of the flying machine?"

She shook her head, frowning. "It was strange. The machine came down, yet Slavers had to go in to get you. As if the ship was empty, except for you. It is a mystery."

Not really, Finn thought. He knew what had happened to the four Slavers who should have been in the ship. And the towering monster must simply have stayed inside the ship until the slaves had been taken back into the Citadel. But he did not waste time explaining all that to Steelfinder.

"How were you taken?" he asked her.

"I was with a group who tried to slip past the whirlsleds coming from the west," she said. "Spywings saw us, and we were attacked. Many died, and many more were injured – and have died here, since then." Her eyes had grown cold as she remembered. "Soon perhaps I too will die, for no slave lives long in the Citadel. I will welcome it."

Finn saw the emptiness in her face, and recognized the fatalism that he had seen before, now and then, in Rainshadow and the other Indians. "Don't be in such a hurry," he said harshly. "Like Baer always says – 'we're not beat till we're dead'."

"Perhaps," Steelfinder said. "But we are slaves. And slaves *are* dead."

Finn sighed, seeing there was no point in arguing. "What surprises me," he said, shifting the subject, "is that the Slavers took you – us – at all. Everyone thought they had come on to the Wasteland to wipe us all out."

"So they have," she said. "But still they need slaves." The corners of her mouth lifted slightly. "The warriors have attacked too many whirlsleds lately. The Citadel has been receiving too few slaves. And it is said that a disease killed many slaves here, weeks ago, before I was taken. So –" She gestured towards the room, more than half-empty.

"Let's hope the Slavers don't get a chance to take any more," Finn growled.

"What of the whirlsled forces on the Wasteland?" Steelfinder asked. "Are they still advancing?"

Finn nodded grimly. "And the people are still retreating. There are thousands of whirlsleds out there now, pushing the people south."

"To the Firesands." Steelfinder sighed faintly. "One way or another, then, it is the end of the Wasteland."

They fell silent for a moment, lost in dark thoughts. Finn was telling himself, as he often had before, that the Wasteland people still had a chance. They might find some way to survive even in that lethal area. They might even find a way across it and out of it again, and so be able to escape the Slaver extermination. It was not much of a hope, but he clung to it – because he so desperately wanted Jena and his friends to live.

And for the same reason, he clung to another hope. He hoped that his friends would think he was dead. Because he knew them – especially Baer. He knew that if they thought he was alive and a slave in the Citadel, they would come and try to get him out. And from all that he had heard about the vast alien fortress, he knew that they could have no hope of succeeding.

He wanted them to stay away. He wanted them to escape the Firesands. He wanted them to live . . .

And then those tormented thoughts fled instantly from his mind. Because the door to the slave chamber had crashed open.

A crowd of hulking, snarling Bloodkin lumbered like great shaggy beasts into the room.

6
Mourning

AS NIGHT DARKENED the rugged folds of the Wasteland, Baer sat on the side of a stony ridge, looking out across the land to the south. On the distant horizon he could see a faint but chilling sight – weird patches that gave off a luminous, greenish-white glow within the midst of the darkness. Baer knew that those patches of land lay within the fearsome Firesands, and that they were only one of the forms of deadliness that existed in that place. But he was not looking at the glow. He was looking inward, at a remembered image that to him was far more monstrous.

The sight of the alien spaceship, lifting off, soon after he and the others had found Josh Ferral. And the sight of the empty land where the ship had been, and where Finn was not to be found.

The loss of Finn had struck them all – perhaps especially Josh – like a crushing club. After a frantic, useless search for their friend, the small group had moved away, northwards, in a heavy and wretched silence. Before long they had met the main body of the Wasteland people, still fleeing south from the advancing Slaver forces. And all of them – after being surprised and pleased at meeting old Josh – had shared the shock and pain and misery at the loss of the young man who had come to mean so much to all of them.

Now, in the depths of the night, the people – more than a

thousand of them – were camped in a secluded canyon below the low ridge where Baer sat. They had made their small fires, and had done the things that needed doing – preparing food, treating big Gratton's injured leg, tending the horses. Then for a time they had sat in their own heavy-hearted silence, as if in mourning.

But they were tough and experienced people, who lived in a world where sudden death and loss were commonplace. They knew they could not mourn for long – not with the advancing hordes of Slavers coming closer, every hour, seeking the final destruction of their Wasteland lives. So, eventually, they began talking among themselves, in low voices.

Now and then some of them might glance up at the silent, brooding figure of Baer, and feel a stab of shared pain. Or they might look with sympathy at old Josh, sitting with Jena, looking empty-eyed and shattered – to have reached his goal after immense suffering, only to find that he had lost his foster son, and that the entire Wasteland was under threat of extinction. But all the same, because of that very threat, it had to be a night of talking, and planning. Their proper mourning, for Finn, would have to wait for another time – if they lived to see such a time.

The talk was mostly led by Corwin, a small, elderly, dark-skinned man who held more knowledge in his bald head than anyone else on the Wasteland. It had been Corwin who had told Rainshadow and the others, when they reached the main body of the people, the blood-chilling news – that the three-sided Slaver force had nearly joined together, to form one long, continuous, curved line of deadly metal. And, worse, that they seemed to be speeding up.

"There can be no doubt, now," Rainshadow said gloomily. "The Slavers mean to drive us into the Firesands."

"It may be so," Corwin said in his quiet voice. "But it may also be that the Slavers believe we will *halt* there, on the edge of the Firesands, and make a stand. When, of course, they would overwhelm us and wipe us out."

Rainshadow looked puzzled. "Why should they think we would stop on the edge?"

"Because," Corwin said, "the Slavers themselves fear the Firesands. The radioactivity is perhaps specially dangerous to them. Certainly we have learned in the past that spywings will not fly over the area. So the Slavers simply may not be able to imagine that *we* would dare to enter the place."

The others nodded slowly, knowing all about the Slavers' lack of imagination, their inability to make intuitive guesses.

"But, Corwin," Jena objected, "you've told us about the time years ago, when The Claw *first* brought an army into the Wasteland, and the people fled into the Firesands. Won't the Slavers remember that, too?"

"No doubt," Corwin said. "But less than half of those people came out again, alive. And by then The Claw's army had withdrawn. It may be that the Slavers did not know that there were *any* survivors."

"I wonder if there will be any this time," Rainshadow murmured. "Especially if the Slavers are bringing their spaceships against us."

"That's an interesting point," Corwin said. "There have been no other sightings of spaceships. And as Baer has confirmed, the ship you saw today was much *smaller* than the great vessels that brought the Slavers to Earth – and that they used against humanity all those centuries ago." He looked around at them brightly, like an enthusiastic teacher in a classroom. "It may be that the ship you saw was on its own, visiting the Wasteland for some other purpose. Certainly the giant ships of the Slaver spacefleet have not been seen in the skies for a very long time."

"Let's hope they won't be, for a lot longer," Jena said, half to herself.

"So, anyway, the Slavers drive us to the Firesands," Marakela put in briskly, "expectin' us t' turn an' fight an' get killed. But we're gonna fool 'em. We're goin' *into* the Firesands – an' get killed there, instead. Right?"

Corwin gave her a fatherly smile. "You could see it like that. And I know, Marakela, that you would prefer to fight. But we truly have a better chance of survival in the Firesands. The people who went in before, those years ago, found a route through all the dangers and horrors. They found it by trial and error, and lost hundreds of people in doing so. But we still know that route, or some of us older ones do. And it leads into the heart of the Firesands, where the Slavers will not dare to follow."

"An' then what?" Marakela demanded.

"Then we will wait," Corwin said heavily. "And we will hope that the Slavers will eventually withdraw, believing us to be dead, as The Claw did on that earlier occasion. And then those of us who have survived the terrors of the Firesands can come out again, and seek a refuge elsewhere."

There was a long silence, as the others pondered Corwin's words, and the cruel choice that awaited them.

"What we need," Jena said at last, almost angrily, "is a route *across* the Firesands, all the way, and out again." She glanced up at the silent figure of Baer. "Preferably towards the west."

Corwin sighed. "I know, and I share your feelings. If Finn is still alive, he will be in the Citadel. But it is a foolish dream to imagine that we could get him out of that fortress. Even if we could get *to* it – which we cannot. There is no route across the Firesands and out again, westward or any other way."

"Y're wrong about that, Mister Corwin."

The flat statement had come from old Josh. And the others turned, startled, and saw that he no longer looked crushed and empty-eyed. He was sitting forward urgently, his leathery face wearing an expression of grim determination.

"There *is* a way," Josh went on, "'cause me an' Gratton came *into* the Firesands from the west. An' out again, t' where Jena an' her friends found us."

As they gaped, he explained. The ferocity of the past winter had forced Josh and Gratton to turn southward, to survive out on the open plains. And later, when they had resumed their route towards the west, they had actually passed many kilometres *south* of the Firesands. Eventually they had come to the foothills of the western mountains, and Josh had realized that they had come too far westwards. So they had turned back, heading northeast in their search for the Wasteland. And that new route had brought them into the Firesands – from the west.

"But, Josh," Corwin said softly, "the dangers that you must have faced . . . There are areas where the sand itself is lethally radioactive. If you crossed any of those, you . . . you could be *dying*, now." He leaned forward, peering into Josh's face. "Have you felt ill? Any nausea, strange aches or pains, numbness in your limbs, hair loss? Anything?"

Josh grinned at him sourly. "I'm an old fella, an' I ache a bit after I've walked 'cross half the country. An' I don't have as much hair as I usedta." The grin faded, and the determined look returned. "But I know what y're talkin' 'bout, Corwin. I had a few books from the Forgotten Time – maybe Finn told y' that – an' I read about this radioactivity stuff. An' I can tell y', I feel fine. Sure, there were places where the land looked funny – kinda *felt* wrong. So we went round 'em. We went round lotsa things."

"The monsters?" Jena said wonderingly. "All those horrors we've heard about?"

"Yep." A shadow passed across Josh's eyes. "Saw some critturs. Saw lotsa things – an' somehow got past 'em. Dunno how, really, now I look back. It's a place more like hell than I ever figgered on seein'. But we just went along – an' got through, by some miracle, or crazy dumb luck."

"And the instincts of a huntsman, perhaps," Corwin said quietly. "Finn always spoke highly of your skills."

The others simply stared at Josh, awe and admiration in their eyes, and a growing, blazing hope. But then a shaggy bulk of muscle pushed its way through the group – and a huge hairy hand fell like a heavy weight on Josh's shoulder.

"I been listenin'," Baer rumbled. "An' if you're up to it, Josh, maybe you could show me this route of yours, to the west. Right about now."

Rainshadow put a restraining hand on Baer's massive arm. "We would all like to take that route, Baer. And we will."

"Like you always say to Finn," Jena added fiercely. "*You're* not going. *We* are."

A murmur of excitement swept through the camp as the nearest warriors, who had heard Josh's words, spread the news. And Corwin's round dark face was beaming.

"It *is* a miracle!" he said. "If Josh can take us across the Firesands, and out again, we can move west and hide ourselves in the foothills – while the Slavers are still waiting, back here, believing that we are all dying inside the Firesands!"

"I c'n get y' across," Josh said firmly. "Only . . ."

"Only we're not *hidin'*," Baer finished for him. "Leastways, I'm not. I'm goin' into the mountains, an' get Finn outa the Citadel. Just like he came to get me, when I was in trouble."

"Now y're talkin', big fella!" Marakela boomed.

Another murmur swept through the people who were crowding around – just as fiercely excited as before, and sounding like wholehearted approval of Baer's words.

But Corwin's eyes were wide and worried. "What are you saying? I love Finn as much as any of you – but how can you hope to rescue him from a huge metal fortress that our weapons could not scratch?"

Baer looked at him grimly. "Remember that I lived in the Citadel. It's open durin' the day, when the Bloodkin take the slaves out. An' there's prob'ly *only* Bloodkin there, now – 'cause the Slavers are out here, tryin' to kill us." He tugged at his vast beard, eyes glinting. "No one's sayin' it'd be easy. But it'd be easier now than if the Slavers were there. If we ride hard, an' get through the Firesands in one piece, we could reach the Citadel in maybe three, four days. I figure Finn's gotta be alive, 'cause he's kinda special to the Slavers. So – we just jump the Bloodkin, fight our way in, an' find him."

"But by then," Corwin persisted, "the whirlsled army will have seen us disappear into the Firesands. By then they might already have turned towards home – the Citadel – believing us to be finished. You could have the whole Slaver force coming down on you!"

"That could happen," Rainshadow said flatly. "You are a wise man, Corwin, and sometimes it is wise to be cautious. But sometimes also, it is unwise not to grasp a chance for victory, when a chance exists. That much at least I have learned from Finn."

"Right!" Marakela boomed. "That wild kid was never *cautious* in his life! An' he'd know that we'll never have a better chance to attack the Citadel, than with the Slavers away from it!"

The murmur of approval, from the crowd of people around, became a yell – sounding very like a battle-cry.

"Perhaps you are right," Corwin said softly. "Perhaps my caution comes from age, not wisdom. And many of us here are alive today only because Finn Ferral was never . . . cautious." He smiled sadly. "So go and do what you must. And I hope for Finn's sake and your own that you will succeed."

Rainshadow rose to his full height, looking around at the warriors. "We will need a fairly strong force, but small enough to be mobile. Not more than three hundred . . ."

His voice was drowned by the clamour, as every able-bodied warrior in the camp began loudly to volunteer. And then, as Rainshadow began the difficult task of selecting the three hundred that would ride to the Citadel, Baer turned to look sombrely at his closest friends.

"I'm glad you're all comin'," he rumbled. "I kinda figured you would. Even though it's gonna be a rough trip, an' a tough fight. Maybe the last fight, for a lotta folks. But we gotta get Finn out."

The great muscles of his chest jumped as he clenched mighty fists. "If we hafta tear the Citadel open with our bare hands."

7
Underground Fortress

"AWRIGHT, WORMS, ON YER FEET!" roared the Bloodkin leader, standing in the centre of the slave chamber. He was as enormously broad as Baer, and his thick matted pelt was a deep and solid black. And his heavy beard was also black, hanging in two separate strands from his massive jaw.

All of the Bloodkin were armed in various ways – long knives or ugly clubs thrust into their belts. But their main weapons looked like nothing more than short, slender rods, held in one hand. Finn had seen those objects in action before – humans called them forcewhips – and he saw them again, now, as the brutal creatures moved among the slaves.

Their sudden growling entry had wakened most of the humans, but some had not risen at once. Then from the ends of the rods in the Bloodkin hands, long orange filaments suddenly sprang out – flexible, glowing strands of fiery energy. The Bloodkin flicked the ends of the filaments at the slower humans, and with yelps and whimpers of pain they sprang up swiftly.

All except one. Across the room, a huddled figure lay still, more unconscious than asleep. And two Bloodkin moved purposefully towards him.

Finn and Steelfinder had got to their feet at the first moment of the Bloodkin's entry. Now they watched grimly as one Bloodkin lashed out with a booted foot. The huddled man on the floor moaned, a sound of pure torment and misery, as the pain dragged him back to semi-consciousness.

Finn's face went cold and hard, and he took a step forward. But Steelfinder grabbed him with surprising strength. "You cannot," she said. "There is nothing you can do."

One of the Bloodkin reached down and effortlessly heaved the moaning man to his feet. He swayed, his skin grey, his face twisted with pain. And then Finn, sickened, saw what was wrong with him. One of his arms was broken, perhaps in more than one place. It had been bound to his side (by Steelfinder, Finn later learned) with a strip of filthy rag, to keep it immobile. But it was hugely swollen, with a puffy bulge where one ragged end of bone was threatening to slice its way through flesh and skin.

"Got us a sick worm," one of the Bloodkin snarled.

"Not much use t' us," the other agreed. "You wanna take him?"

The first Bloodkin grinned and nodded, and roughly pushed the injured man towards the door. The man cried out as his shattered arm was jolted – but the Bloodkin merely laughed, and pushed him again.

A blind rage took hold of Finn, and again he began to step forward. But again Steelfinder was in the way, strong fingers digging painfully into his arm. "Finn," she hissed, "if you drive them into a rage, they will whip you till you are dead. I say to you what you said to me – do not be in a hurry to die!"

The words penetrated Finn's rage, and held him back. Sickened and agonized by his own helplessness, and by the depths of misery around him, he turned away. And found himself staring at a vast breadth of muscle covered in coal-black hair.

The forcewhip glimmered orange in the Bloodkin leader's hand. "You two," he snarled. "Move!"

"Careful, Forkbeard," another Bloodkin called mockingly. "Them two is wild worms, from the desert."

"Not wild now," growled the leader, Forkbeard. "Jus' worms with work t' do, like the rest."

Battling against his inner storm of rage and revulsion, Finn turned away towards the door through which the man with the broken arm had been taken by his Bloodkin guard. In that instant, from the corridor outside, he heard a high, agonized shriek from the injured man – an echoing shriek that seemed to fill the corridor, until at last it faded, and died away.

That scream stayed with Finn for most of the day, and acted within him like fuel to the fire of his rage and hate. Yet it was a cold fire, controlled and hard, that seemed to give him extra strength and alertness.

The other humans – except for the calm, quiet Steelfinder – had paid absolutely no attention to the new slave in their midst. If any of them looked directly at Finn, it was with blank, unseeing eyes. They all seemed to be wrapped in a haze of numb apathy, like the walking dead.

They had all been there for some time, Finn knew – longer even than Steelfinder. And they also all came from lives far different from those of the Wasteland warriors. These people had lived in the huddled crude villages where most humans lived – where life was pinched and dreary and miserable, and where everyone was permanently, inescapably afraid, unable to forget the presence of the unknowable aliens who ruled the Earth. So now, as slaves, with that fear having become an even worse reality, they had withdrawn into themselves, into a mindless empty place that offered a kind of relief from that unbearable reality. They shuffled and shambled, heads down, moving like robots where and how the Bloodkin told them. It was a normal human reaction to shock and horror and total hopelessness.

But Finn Ferral was not a normal human. He had proved that when he had set out to do the impossible, to free his family from the Slavers. And now that he himself was a slave, he had no intention of sinking into blank-eyed apathy. Once again he was determined to do the impossible – and free himself.

So he studied his surroundings carefully, as the Bloodkin marched the group of slaves through the Citadel. Over the months Baer had told him much about the vast structure, and now he could see the details for himself. And any one of those details might offer him a clue, an edge of a chance.

He knew that, like all Slaver centres, the Citadel was mostly underground. Baer had said that there were five levels, and only the topmost level was above the surface of the earth. And that top level held the only entrance – one enormous doorway, wide enough for whirlsleds to enter two abreast.

Finn also knew that the slave chamber was on the lowest level. And the quarters of the Bloodkin – some five hundred of the hairy beast-men lived in the Citadel – were on the level above. Scattered through those two levels, also, were some of the strange machines that kept the Citadel running – including the power source. It provided the inner illumination, among other things – the dim glow that came directly from the metal walls.

Outside the slave chamber, the group of humans was driven along a narrow corridor, with blank metal walls, twisting and oddly angled. Finn knew that every level of the Citadel was a tangle of such corridors, branching and interweaving, with connecting rooms and chambers opening from them. It was all like a gigantic ants' nest, but far more complex, and totally unsymmetrical in the alien way.

As they moved around one of the angled corners, Finn saw a strange yellow glow ahead. It was like a pillar of light, stretching from the floor to a broad, almost circular opening in the ceiling. And Finn recognized it from the other Slaver base that he had entered months before. The yellow light was a strange kind of force, like an elevator between the levels.

A few at a time, the slaves were herded into the light – where they floated upwards, eerily, as the strange force lifted them to the next level. When Finn had gone up in his turn, the stink of the next level, the Bloodkin quarters, nearly choked him. But at once they were moved on to another of the yellow columns of light, and were wafted up again – to the third level, at the centre of the Citadel.

This, Finn knew, was the mystery level.

According to Baer, there was an area in the centre of the third level that was kept mysteriously locked and secret. Not even Bloodkin were allowed in that sanctum. That had always annoyed Baer, whose extra share of humanity had given him a thirst for knowledge and a healthy human curiosity. So Finn gazed round with interest.

And he wondered – could this level, with its secret sanctum, have something to do with the metal-suited giant from the spaceship?

But the Bloodkin hurried the group on even faster. Soon they were rising up to the second level, where the Slavers kept more machinery and strange devices – including the equipment they used for mining human metals, that had survived, buried, from the Forgotten Time. Then at last they reached the top level, and the ragged group shuffled away along more twisting, angled corridors, the Bloodkin barking and snarling around them.

By then most people would have been hopelessly lost, in that mazy network of criss-crossing corridors and weird elevators. But Finn knew that he could find his way back to the slave chamber along precisely the route they had followed. He had a wild creature's directional sense – and he also had his sense of smell, with which he could have tracked back, following the odour of the humans, like a hunting dog on the trail.

But he had no wish to retrace his steps just then. Ahead, he saw a blaze of light from the great doorway that was the Citadel's only entrance. They were going outside – where there would be light, fresh air, and also perhaps more chances for someone like himself to find a way to freedom.

"Got new work fer y' t'day, worms," one of the Bloodkin sniggered. "Y' better be feelin' strong."

Finn ignored him, not knowing or caring what work the slaves would be forced to do. All he wanted then, all that every wilderness instinct within him clamoured for, was to be out in the open air.

The shambling crowd moved out through the vast doorway, blinking in the sunlight. And Finn, gratefully filling his lungs with cool mountain air, turned to look at the structure.

It was truly enormous, by far the largest building that Finn had ever seen. Not that it rose high above him, since only one of its levels was visible on the surface. But it spread over an immense breadth, an area four times larger than the full extent of the forest village where Finn had lived. It was vaguely an oval shape, though as usual not symmetrical, and its solid blank walls held the dark gleam of alien metal.

Finn continued to look around as the column of slaves moved away. The Citadel had been built on a slight rise of land in the middle of a broad plateau. The land of the plateau was slightly rolling, open and grassy, except for some small thickets of shrubbery dotted here and there across it. It seemed to be at least three kilometres across. And all around it, as if the plateau was the bottom of a giant granite bowl, rose the titanic, rock-slabbed slopes of the western mountains.

It *is* a fortress, Finn thought numbly. Protected by the mountains that surround it, and by the solid rock that most of it is buried in, and by the no less solid metal of the walls on the topmost level. No one could get in there, once that huge door was closed.

And again, he whispered within himself that fierce hope – that his friends would think he was dead, so that they would not take the suicidal risk of trying to rescue him.

By then the cavalcade of slaves had been herded around to the north side of the huge structure. On that side the plateau stretched out even farther, ending in what looked like steep cliffs. There, too, the ground seemed more level than on the rest of the plateau, and grass grew only sparsely on it. And Finn saw that there were places where the bare ground looked scorched and burnt, and where craters and deep gouges had been carved into the earth and the rock beneath it.

He saw all that at a glance. But his gaze was caught and held by what he saw, squatting evilly, at the edge of the level area. The contorted oval shape of the spaceship that had held the giant alien monster.

The door of the ship was closed, and it looked silent and deserted. So probably, Finn thought, the towering being was inside the Citadel. But as Finn studied the ship, a peculiarity struck him.

It looked almost small, sitting alone on the edge of the wide level stretch of land. And beneath it were small scorch marks, and a slight crumbling of the soil. But those marks were nowhere near as large or widespread as the other gouges and gashes across the area.

Finn suddenly remembered that Baer had spoken of gigantic spaceships, far bigger than the one he had entered. Was this flat area the place where such ships landed?

And if so – where were they now?

"Do not let them see you looking around so much," whispered Steelfinder, at his side. "They will . . . *uh*!"

It was a grunt of pain – and in the same instant Finn felt a lancing stab of fire in his own back. He whirled, and was again facing the vast, black-furred bulk of the Bloodkin called Forkbeard – who had flicked his forcewhip across their backs.

"Shuddup, worms, an' move," Forkbeard growled. "Got diggin' t' do. Gon' be *earth*worms, you."

He roared with laughter at his own joke. But at the same time his small, deep-set eyes were watching Finn, seeing the clenched fists, the muscles jumping in the jaw. The bellowing laughter faded, and one black-haired hand took a firmer grip on the forcewhip, while the other slid to the heavy, metalheaded club at his belt.

"Finn!" Steelfinder said, in a low but sharp voice.

And again Finn saw that what he wanted to do, with every cell of his being – to leap at the hairy throat of Forkbeard – would be senseless, and hopeless. He forced himself to relax, to let his eyes drop. And then he turned away, as ugly Bloodkin laughter rose all around him, to begin his first day as a slave.

8
Firesands

BAER WHEELED HIS horse swiftly, as a warrior's cry of warning was drowned by an outburst of harsh and chilling howls.

The small army that Rainshadow had gathered was carefully skirting a broad patch of brush – a tangled mass of branches that seemed almost tied in knots, covered in a pasty green powdery substance, like mould. The horses had been nervous, but then they had been that way for nearly every moment of that day. And then the pack of creatures had erupted from the brush.

They were the size of very large dogs, but with extra-long, powerful hind legs and two pairs of shorter forelegs. Their skin was a scaly green-grey, and their mouths were crammed with curved black fangs. There were about a hundred of the monsters in the pack, and they flung themselves at the riders with fearless savagery.

But the instant's warning was all the warriors needed. The leading creatures were still in mid-leap, fanged mouths gaping, when they were transfixed by slim spears hurled with deadly accuracy. Baer's hand swept up with startling speed to draw his machete, and chopped down furiously at another leaping monster, slicing it almost in two. And Jena, Marakela and the rest of the warriors had moved as quickly – and the other beasts fell, bristling with arrows, staining the sand with purplish blood.

Baer watched the warriors dismount to reclaim their spears and arrows. "Don't bother cuttin' any steaks," he said, with a ghost of his usual crooked grin. "Nobody's that hungry."

The ripple of laughter among the warriors was as muted and wry as Baer's smile. And that smile faded as Baer glanced over at Jena and Josh. They were riding double, since Josh was no horseman – but they were both light, and the muscular young horse seemed untroubled.

"You two all right?" Baer asked.

"Yep," Josh replied. His lined face seemed even more drawn with weariness and tension, but the determined light still shone brightly in his eyes. "This pesky crittur don't seem made fer sittin'," he went on, patting the horse's solid haunch. "But it's better'n walkin'."

"Sure is, in this place," Baer said grimly. "Where now?"

Josh pointed to a rocky ridge in the distance, bare and white as bone. "We follow that ridge a ways. Hafta watch out fer the vines."

"What *don't* we hafta watch out for?" Baer growled, as they urged their horses forward again.

The vines turned out to be long snaky tendrils, thick as a man's wrist, lying mostly unseen just below the surface of the sand – but thrusting up evilly sharp thorns that would impale the feet of any unwary passing creature. The riders kept well away, hardly even glancing at the tendrils. Though they were only about halfway through the first day of their journey, they had grown almost used to the catalogue of mutant horrors that lay along the tortuous route that Josh had found.

They had seen gigantic cacti, bulging horribly like over-filled balloons, with long thorns the rusty-red colour of dried blood. Distorted shrubs that had neither leaves nor bark, but were covered with a glistening, putrid slime. Plants with broad leaves curved like bowls, from which viscous liquid slowly dripped, hissing like acid as it struck the ground.

They had passed areas where the soil itself was in constant

motion, as if unseen things burrowed just beneath the surface. They had circled round patches of sand that glittered greenish-white – perhaps, Baer thought, the sources of that evil luminous glow, at night. They had avoided other stretches of land that looked like lakes – but lakes of crude and rippled glass, made when the sand was fused by some unimaginable heat.

They had bypassed a broad, shallow basin filled a metre deep with fine white ash, where smoke and foul gases seeped from cracks in the earth. They had halted briefly, their way blocked by a moving carpet of small slithering things, eyeless and legless, covered with needle-sharp spines and stinking like dead fish.

And they had broken into a frantic gallop at the sight, in the distance, of something that looked like a lizard, with a crest of sharp horns on its head and along its spine. Except that it had twice the number of legs that a normal lizard has, and was five times bigger than the biggest horse.

But aside from that one wild dash, the small army kept to an easy, steady canter, which ate up the distance without exhausting the sturdy mustangs. They paused only briefly now and then, for a gulp of water and a mouthful of dried meat. But all the time, as they rode, they left clear markings along their trail.

For the rest of the Wasteland people – including the young, the old, the disabled, protected by the remaining warriors – were following more slowly along Josh's route. Once out of the Firesands, that main body of people, as planned, would swing into the foothills, to seek a refuge and hiding place. But the three hundred warriors of the small army would by then be in the mountains, moving towards the Citadel.

Providing, Baer thought sourly, we ever *do* get out of this place. Josh had been telling the simple truth when he described the Firesands as hellish. And Baer had not stopped marvelling at the skill and luck and sheer grit that had brought the old man through, on foot, and part of the time with a wounded companion.

At least the horses were carrying the army through the region a good deal more quickly. And that speed kept them out of trouble more than once, as that first day wore on. Yet as one ghastliness followed another, it began to feel to Baer and the others that the day would go on forever.

Until at last Josh raised a weary hand and pointed to the horizon. Squinting, Baer could see a group of tall spires, carved from naked rock by the gritty wind, stark and thin as skeletons.

"Past there," Josh said, "things get better. If we keep goin' at this rate, we should be outa the Firesands 'fore midnight."

Baer grunted gratefully, but Jena looked with concern at her father. "We should stop awhile before then," she said. "You could do with a rest."

"Perhaps once we are out, Josh," Rainshadow said, "you should stay behind, and wait for Corwin and the others to come along."

Josh shook his grizzled head firmly. "I'm not that tired. Not that old, neither." The fierce light flared brighter in his eyes. "My boy came t' get me when I was a slave. I aim t' be there when you folks go t' get him."

For Finn, as for the warriors in the Firesands, that day – the first day of his enslavement – seemed to go on forever. It was a day of back-breaking drudgery, on the crudest level. The slaves had to bring earth and rock, from elsewhere on the plateau, to fill the craters and gouges in the broad level area. With no tools, they dug with their bare hands, and used their own shirts and tunics like stretchers to carry the loads.

Most of the humans, having been slaves for weeks or months, were thin and starved and weak. They staggered and stumbled, often falling with exhaustion – only to be brutally whipped to their feet by the Bloodkin. Even Finn, young and fit and muscular, was soon sweating and panting, his fingers raw from the primitive digging. But even so he took every chance to study his surroundings, looking and learning.

He had seen, early in the day, a fold between two uprearing mountain flanks, on the eastern edge of the plateau. It had to be a pass, leading out through the peaks – no doubt the route taken by whirlsleds, coming and going. But it would be the most obvious, and least safe, route for a fleeing slave. So his eyes searched the cracks and creases of the almost sheer slopes that surrounded the plateau, for other routes. Just as they also examined every rock and bush on the plateau itself, which might offer cover that would allow him to vanish, completely and suddenly, given the edge of a chance.

But there were no chances. The Bloodkin guards were alert and watchful – and Forkbeard, their blackfurred leader, was never more than two strides away from Finn. That was probably, Finn guessed, because he was a new slave, still healthy, and a slave from the Wasteland, all the more likely to try to break away.

Eventually, the sun crept slowly down past the western peaks, and the exhausted slaves were herded back to the Citadel, stumbling through all the corridors down to the slave chamber. There in the open doorway were two crude metal containers – one holding scummy water, the other holding a thin stew with the texture and taste of mud. The slaves found energy enough to jostle and push to get at the filthy food. And though the smell of the stuff nauseated Finn, he pushed and shoved for his own share. He did not intend to be too weak from hunger to take any chance for escape that might come along.

Soon afterwards, the slaves were sinking to the floor, almost instantly asleep, not even noticing as the heavy door slid shut. But Finn joined Steelfinder at the side of the room. She was sitting against the wall, staring straight ahead, a haunted look in her dark eyes.

"What is it?" Finn asked concernedly, crouching beside her.

She turned her head slowly. "I was thinking of Keller – the man with the broken arm," she said. "A good man, friendly and harmless. But there is no place here for a slave who cannot work." Her mouth set in a hard line. "Keller has found the only release there can be, from here."

For a moment the two of them sat in gloomy silence. Then Finn stirred, trying to shake off the depression that was settling on him. "Steelfinder, there are things I need to know. Can you tell me where the young women slaves are – the girls?"

"There are none," she told him bleakly. "There were a few, in the place where the Slavers do cruel things to them, but I heard the Bloodkin say they had died from the disease I told you of. Since then, the whirlsleds have been on the Wasteland, and no new slaves have come except for you and me."

Finn felt deep relief. But he still had other questions. "How many Slavers," he asked, "have stayed behind, in the Citadel?"

"Only a few," Steelfinder told him. "Perhaps two dozen. But we see little of them." She looked at him intently. "Are you asking me these questions because you still have foolish thoughts of escaping?"

Finn returned her gaze steadily. "They're not foolish. There has to be a way. And when I find it, I'll take you with me – and these poor creatures, if I can." He smiled faintly. "I owe you that much, for your kindness to me."

Steelfinder did not return the smile. "It is a good thought, and I thank you," she said gravely. "But it is still a young man's foolishness. There is no way out. Except the way that Keller found."

She turned away, seeking a place on the floor to sleep. And Finn too settled himself on the bare metal, for the night. But as he waited for sleep to come, his jaw was set firm, and his eyes were hard.

She's wrong, he told himself. There has to be a way. There *has* to.

The morning brought another slow march up through the Citadel's maze of corridors, and another day's crushing, pain-filled drudgery on the level area of the plateau. And then that day ended, with the shambling return to the slave chamber, and more of the foul food. And another day followed, and after that another – all of a mind-crippling, deadening sameness.

But, on that fifth day, a small variation entered into the dismal progress of time. It happened when Forkbeard drove Finn and another slave to a spot slightly farther from the edge of the level area, to gather up some of a clutter of broken rock. To reach that spot, they had to pass by one of the dense thickets of shrubbery on the plateau. And as they did so, Finn's nostrils flared.

An odd flow of air seemed to be coming from the thicket, as if the bushes were creating a breeze. An unnaturally *warm* breeze.

And the flow of warm air carried a peculiar odour – a scent that lifted the hair on Finn's neck with its strangeness, yet one that he had experienced once before . . .

Desperately, he wanted to explore the thicket. But Forkbeard still hovered close by, and there was no chance – until several hours had passed. By then, a chill rain had begun to fall, and the bare earth grew slippery and treacherous. The other weary slave working with Finn fell heavily, and did not rise quickly enough.

Forkbeard's forcewhip sizzled in the rain as he struck at the fallen man. Crying out, the man rolled away, scrambling to avoid the lashing filament. And Forkbeard, roaring with rage, lumbered in pursuit. For a moment, Finn was alone.

He might then have simply fled, vanishing into cover as only he could do. But he had been helped, when he had first arrived, by the brave and thoughtful kindness of Steelfinder, and he would not try to escape without her – or without the other wretched slaves, if possible.

So, instead, he stepped backwards, into the nearby thicket.

The warm flow of air that carried the strange scent led him to its source in a few quick strides. And there he halted, while joy and hope and puzzlement mingled within him.

It looked like the mouth of a tunnel – a not-quite-circular hole in the side of a mound of earth. It had a heavy grating over it, made of criss-crossed bars of sturdy metal. And from it gushed the warm air, with that peculiar but familiar smell.

The tunnel had to lead out of the Citadel. And if he could somehow get out of the slave chamber, and find the tunnel's other end, inside the structure . . .

But still he was puzzled, because he could not work out what the tunnel was. It was not a form of ventilation, for it poured air *out* rather than taking it in. Anyway, the Citadel could not be said to be ventilated – the air on the lower levels was stifling and foul. So why was this warm air being forced out from somewhere within the fortress?

And the odour . . . Why, he wondered, should the flow of air carry with it the same disturbing, sickly smell that he had first sensed when he had crept into the alien spaceship?

He stepped forward, took hold of the grating, and tugged. But it was solid, its metal edges embedded in solid rock. He released his grip, thinking hard.

And then a ferocious roar sounded almost in his ear. And a huge, hairy, rain-wet hand grasped him by the arm and flung him away.

"You gon' get a whippin', worm!" Forkbeard bellowed. "Sneakin' away . . .!"

Finn had half-fallen into the dripping shrubbery. But he found his feet at once, bracing himself as the huge Bloodkin advanced, forcewhip flickering.

But then Forkbeard stopped, and his small eyes widened. He was staring at Finn with astonishment. But he was not looking at Finn's face.

Finn glanced down, and icy shock swept through him. The drenching rain had begun to wash away the dirt and dried blood that had masked the pattern of dark dots on his upper left arm. And the rough grasp of Forkbeard's wet hand, on that arm, had completed the job. The pattern was clearly visible.

"Y're ... *that* one!" the Bloodkin said in a startled growl. "The wild worm – the killer from the forest in the east!"

Finn crouched, in near panic, a wild beast at bay. But before he could move, other huge, shaggy forms crashed into the thicket. At a barked command from Forkbeard, they rushed at Finn. He struggled furiously, striking and kicking, but their vast weight bore him to the ground, and their sharp knives were at his throat.

"Don' kill him!" Forkbeard bellowed. "Don' even hurt him much!" He grinned, a brutal flash of yellow fangs. "We gon' t' celebrate t'night! We jus' caught us a worm that the Masters've wanted caught fer most of a year!"

9
Heart of the Citadel

FORKBEARD AND THREE other Bloodkin dragged Finn back to the Citadel, his arms twisted painfully behind his back. Once inside the great entrance, Forkbeard hurried away to take the news to the Slavers. Finn still struggled, snarling like an enraged panther, but the huge Bloodkin kept their grip on him as easily as adults would hold a child.

Then Forkbeard hurried back, with two Slavers. The aliens were not armed, but then they had no need to carry heatlances within the safe walls of their fortress. They examined Finn's arm, their yellow eyes shifting to a pale blue-green. Then they burst into a stream of their strangled, clicking, gargling language – and Forkbeard replied, in a guttural version of the same sounds.

In a moment they were joined by two more Slavers, bringing with them a strange object. It looked like a large box, with transparent walls and lid, about a metre and a half high, two metres long. And it rested on a disc of shiny metal that hovered slightly from the floor, as a whirlsled would hover. The aliens gargled and clicked at one another again, then one of them spoke briefly to Forkbeard. And the dark-furred Bloodkin leered savagely at Finn.

"Masters want me t' tell y'," he growled, "don' touch the sides of this thing. If y' do, it'll hurt real bad. Unnerstand?"

Finn merely glared, baring his teeth in another snarl. But

then he saw one Slaver carefully press a small indentation at the side of the case. The lid opened silently, and a Bloodkin lifted Finn and dumped him inside.

As the lid closed, Finn realized that the transparent top and sides were not made of glass or plastic. There was a faint hazy sparkle in them – like the energy screen that covered the door of the slave chamber. They admitted air and sound as well as light. And they were *warm* – already beginning to dry his rain-wet clothes.

The four Slavers stalked away, the hovering disc carrying Finn, in the weird box, along with them. Finn studied his alien cage more closely. He was aware of the many strange energies that the Slavers controlled – in the whirlsleds, the Citadel's elevators, and so on. But he knew nothing of how such devices worked. And he could not quite believe that the aliens could make a *cage*, a seemingly solid box, out of a form of energy.

So, his curiosity once again getting the better of his caution, he reached out with a fingertip and touched one side of his cage.

It was like being struck by lightning. A blaze of searing agony stabbed into his skin, and flashed through his body. He could not pull his finger away. He jerked and twisted in a terrible convulsion, and his mouth stretched wide in a noiseless scream of pain.

Instantly the Slavers halted the hovering disc, and opened the lid of the cage. One of them reached in, its claws gripping Finn's jerkin – careful not to touch his flesh – and dragged him roughly away from the cage's side.

The pain vanished at once, leaving behind only its searing memory. It also left Finn shaky and trembling. But within seconds the trembling faded, as his heartbeat and breathing returned to normal. He lay back carefully in the centre of the cage floor, as the Slavers strode on through the corridors.

Within a few moments, they came to one of the strange elevators, which lowered Finn's cage and his alien guards down to the next level. After another series of twisting corridors, they floated down again on another elevator. That meant that they were on the third, central level of the Citadel. The mystery level.

Within Finn a knot of anticipation formed. The Slavers might be taking him to their private area – that secret, central sanctum where even Bloodkin were not allowed. For a moment he did not even think about how much more impossible it would be to try to escape from such a place. His chronic curiosity was again stirring within him.

There were many mysteries surrounding the Slavers that no human, not even Corwin, had been able to solve. And then there was the newer mystery – of the towering, metal-suited monster. If answers to those mysteries existed anywhere, they might lie within the Citadel sanctum that the aliens kept so secret.

Anticipation grew within him as they moved at last along a corridor that was wider than usual, and that ended in a broad, high metal door. Most doors in Slaver structures had small touch-panels beside them, to open or close them. But this one had no such panel. So Finn watched intently as one Slaver reached up to the top edge of the door.

On the smooth blank metal there was an almost invisible depression, which even Finn's keen eyes might not have detected. But he fixed the spot in his mind as the Slaver's claw touched it, and the door slid silently open.

The disc carrying the energy cage drifted forward. And the anticipation within Finn turned to sick and appalled revulsion.

It was one of the aliens' weird laboratories. A long, broad room, with an enormous flat slab of metal like a table-top standing in the centre, supported by a solid central pillar. There were oddly-shaped tools and implements scattered on the slab, and banks of strange, brightly lit machinery surrounding it.

But Finn only glanced at those things. His stricken gaze had swung to the large transparent containers standing on more of the table-like slabs, all around the chamber. They were filled with liquid – a clear liquid, that let Finn see what it was that floated in the containers.

Corpses – of an enormous variety of beasts. Most of them were ugly Wasteland mutations, including some that Finn had never seen. Some were animals from other parts of the country, which he recognized. A few were creatures that were strangely shaped, not familiar to Finn, but which he guessed were from other parts of the world rather than mutations.

All floated silently, suspended in the liquid, staring sightlessly through dead eyes. Then, in some containers in a more central position, Finn saw a sight that made him flinch as if he had been struck.

Whoever or whatever had created this grisly array of preserved corpses had included *human* bodies within it. Men and women of all ages and sizes, also floating in clear liquid, like specimens gathered by some evil scientific collector. Finn realized that they were all probably the bodies of dead slaves – because he recognized one of them. Keller, the man with the broken arm, who had been taken from the slave chamber four days earlier.

Swallowing hard against the acid bite of nausea in his throat, Finn turned his head to watch as the aliens moved to one of the several doors that opened out of that gruesome chamber. This door, being inside the secret sanctum, had an ordinary touchpanel to open it. And it slid open to reveal another laboratory, filled with more hideous sights.

But these sights did not appal or sicken Finn so much. He was looking at beings who were clearly dead – but with a jolt of astonishment he saw that they had never been truly alive.

On another of the heavy metal slabs, he saw a few of the bat-shaped bodies of spywings, glassy eyes bulging. Their bodies had also been split open, and Finn could see rods and discs and other metallic shapes glinting amid the green-tinged flesh. But that sight did not surprise him. He had brought down many spywings, with his unerring sling, and had long known that the creatures were an uncanny mixture of flesh and metal. The surprise came as his cage moved farther into the chamber.

A great many smaller versions of the slab-tables stood there, surrounded by more complex machinery. On those platforms, Slavers lay – limp and dead, with blank colourless eyes. And the bulging torso of each silent alien body – the torso with its hard armour that even heatlances could not pierce – had somehow, like the spywings, been *opened.*

It was as if a panel had been removed, from the front. And Finn saw the glistening inner flesh, the weirdly twisted and coiled alien organs, bathed in the green slime that was the creatures' blood.

But he also saw the other things. Curved rods and distorted cones and tangles of fine filaments . . . Those things, too, were awash in the green slime. But through it, unmistakably, they showed the gleam of shiny metal.

So at last Finn knew that the guess he had made, at the beginning of his quest, had been correct. The Slavers *were* like the spywings. They were not truly living things. They were *made.*

But that led again to the question that Corwin had once put into words. If the Slavers were made – then who, or what, made them?

The question still echoed in Finn's mind as the energy cage was moved on by its four guards. Yet his alertness did not slacken, as they passed through more of the large rooms. And Finn understood that the secret sanctum was a collection of interconnecting chambers, each with several doors, all forming a sort of circular shell around some central core.

In two further chambers, he saw no more creatures – just more banks and batteries of strange machines. But in another room, he saw a dozen Slavers – standing before twelve strangely flickering screens, with ghostly shapes on them.

And when Finn realized what those shapes were, he came near to burning himself again on the energy cage. The screens were showing images of the Wasteland's broken, rocky terrain – towering, swirling clouds of dust – and, barely visible, small egg-shapes moving along the ground.

Finn had not recognized the shapes at once because he had never before seen them from that angle. From high in the sky, where the spywings swooped, their bulging eyes transmitting the images of what they saw back to the Slavers' screens.

The cage drifted past quickly, and Finn nearly cried out. He wanted to look again at the pictures, which showed the Slavers' remorseless, scouring march across the Wasteland. He wanted to see if there were humans in those pictures – fleeing, or fighting, or dying . . .

But his cage had left the screens behind, as it floated on the hovering disc into yet another room. This one was also large and bright, with more strange machines and instruments scattered around on slab-tables. Yet there were differences, and Finn stared round at them intently.

For one thing, this room had another glowing screen, embedded in the wall at one end. But this screen, far larger than the twelve others he had seen, held no images – merely a dull greenish glow.

For another thing, the air in this room was different. Though Finn remained warm inside the energy cage, he could sense that the room beyond the cage was bitterly cold, nearly at freezing point, and heavy with moisture.

And, for a third thing, he could hear a quiet hum within the room. He looked up – and had to clench his teeth to hold back a shout of exultation.

Halfway up one of the walls was an opening, a dark gap, not quite a circle, covered with a grating of criss-crossed strips of metal. Like the tunnel mouth that he had found in the thicket, on the plateau.

This cold, damp, inner chamber held the tunnel's other end.

The hum came from just behind the grating. Finn knew nothing about air-conditioning, but he dimly grasped the idea that some machine was pouring the cold wet air into the room – and, at the same time, from its other side, was expelling a stream of warm air. The warm flow that he had detected in the thicket.

He leaned back, forcing himself to relax. It could be his way out, he knew. But not while he was trapped inside a deadly energy cage, guarded by Slavers.

By then his captors were guiding the disc on to one of the slab-tables. So they had brought him to his destination, he thought. Wherever that was.

Behind him, he heard another door open, across the room from the door he had been brought through. He began to turn to see what was happening. As he did so, he heard a strange burst of sound. Something like the clicking, gargling speech of the Slavers, but softer and more liquid, more of a bubbling or gobbling sound.

By then he had turned far enough to see. And every atom of blood in his veins seem to turn to solid ice.

Unbelievable, mind-crumpling horror had stalked into the room.

10
Cacinnix

THE HORROR LOOMED over Finn, standing more than four metres tall. And only that, and the heavy, sickly odour of it, told Finn that it was the metal-suited monster from the spaceship.

It was no longer wearing that suit – but Finn, in the grip of terror and loathing, deeply wished that it was. It was wearing a kind of short robe of shiny cloth, which left its long thin arms and legs bare, and its chest and throat as well. Its flesh was hairless, a deathly grey, and its skin was wrinkled and creased – seeming to droop and hang from its long skinny frame in baggy folds. And the skin was wet and glistening, covered with a coat of thick, reeking liquid that slid and oozed among the folds.

Its long head was also hairless, with drooping slime-wet skin. There were no ears, and only two deeper creases that might have been nostrils. And there was a wide lipless slash of a mouth, and large rectangular eyes – glowing a lurid yellow, but shifting in colour to a watery blue as they stared down at Finn.

And Finn, glaring upwards in his frozen horror, numbly understood that he was looking at the being, or one of the beings, that had made the Slavers. Monsters from another world, who had created their partly mechanical servants to some extent in the image of their makers.

The monster drew back, looming more than twice the height of the Slavers, and spoke in its rasping, gobbling tones. The four

Slavers turned and marched silently out of the room. Then the towering, wrinkled being moved to one of the other slab-tables. Still making the gobbling sound – as if muttering to itself – it picked something up in one of its long, three-fingered hands, and crossed the room towards yet another of the unknown alien machines. Finn saw that the object it was carrying was a small, shiny metal sphere. It dropped the sphere into a slot in the machine, and ran its fingers over a succession of switches. Then it stepped back, and spoke again.

But this time Finn scarcely heard the burst of gobbling. Because, at almost the same instant, the *machine* spoke – in Finn's own language.

"Speak now, little creature," it said.

Finn goggled, his skin crawling with the eerie, incomprehensible shock of those words. Again the monster spoke; again, a fraction of a second later, the machine also spoke.

"You must speak. The machine is tuned to your primitive noises. You have not died. You *must* speak, little rat. *Speak.*"

Still Finn simply stared, his mind unable to come to terms with the impossibility of what was happening.

Again the monster gobbled, followed at once by words from the machine.

"Will this one be like the others after all?" it said. "Its small mind broken, its heart bursting from terror? But this one is the special one, bred alive in the laboratories of the east. It is braver and cleverer than the rest. It cannot die of fear. It *must* speak. Speak, little one, *speak*!"

Slowly, as if it weighed a ton, Finn turned his head away from the machine, and looked at the monster. And though most technology was a mystery to him, he began – dimly, as if through a veil – to understand.

Somehow, when the monster made its gobbling sounds, the machine was *translating* them – speaking them again, in Finn's language.

And the giant alien wanted Finn to reply.

The words came unbidden, automatically, to his lips. And of all the things he might have said, the words arose not out of his fear or horror or shock, but out of his curiosity.

"What . . ." he whispered, haltingly. "What *are* you?"

The monster lurched forward, with a weird kind of whistling yelp. The pale blue of the eyes shifted, ending in a startling orange. And a torrent of the gobbling speech poured from the lipless mouth.

"It is! It is true! It is proved! You *can* speak! Excellent little rat – speak again! Talk!"

"I don't know . . ." Finn said, still haltingly, "what you want of me."

Again the whistling yelp came, and Finn's numbed mind vaguely thought that it must be the alien's version of a cry of joy.

"I want proof!" the giant said, through the metallic voice of the machine. "I want to prove what I have long believed – that you and your kind *do* have a small, crude intelligence of a sort!"

Finn stared, nervously, as the monster bent down towards the cage.

"Do you understand? Probably not. Yet you have not died of fear at the sight of me, as many of your kind do. And you have shown that you can speak – and so perhaps can have some glimmer of understanding. Is that not so, little rat?"

Through the blank numbness caused by so much shock and fear, Finn began to feel a surge of anger. "I'm no rat," he muttered. "I'm a human being – a man."

The giant alien turned to stare at the machine. "How odd," he said, through the translation. "You have just said that you are not a rat, but that instead you are a rat. It makes no sense. Perhaps your mind is more limited than I thought. Or perhaps the translator finds difficulty dealing with such a primitive language." Again, the long fingers touched buttons, rippled over switches. "Speak again. Tell me if your kind has reached the level where you have names for one another. Have you a name, little rat?"

The anger was growing within Finn. Clearly the machine had no other word for "man", in the monster's language, but "rat". That was because it was the monster's machine – and the creature saw humans as merely vermin.

As the anger grew, Finn's shocked numbness began rapidly to fade. "Finn," he growled. "My name is Finn."

Another whistling yelp. "You do! I can hardly believe it! You can speak, you can think to some extent, you have a name! It is *proved*!"

He bent nearer. "Speak again, little Finn. Tell me of yourself, what you do out in the place of hot sands. Speak."

Finn merely glared. This is impossible, he began to think. Perhaps it's a dream, some kind of delirium. Perhaps I'm insane, or dying, and not really here talking to a horror from another world.

"You have nothing to say?" the monster went on, through the machine. "But of course. You are a small, primitive creature, confused and fearful. I can hardly expect conversation." The eyes shifted colour again, to a molten turquoise. "Perhaps you will speak more when you have grown used to me. Meanwhile, *I* shall talk to *you*. You may even understand a little of what I say."

And so the monster continued, in the same rambling stream of talk. It was rather as a person might chat idly to his pet dog or cat – or, perhaps, even to a rat he had caught in a trap. And Finn listened, fascinated, for he was hearing answers to questions that humans had been asking for centuries.

Finn learned that the monster was called Cacinnix, of a race known as the Vlantis, taking their name from their faraway planet, Vlant. Cacinnix was the Controller sent to oversee operations on Earth. He did not spend all his time on Earth, but came now and then for a prolonged visit – remaining in the Citadel, within the central sanctum, where his rooms were kept cold and damp like the atmosphere of his world. But sometimes he ventured out – in his protective metal suit – to pursue his hobby. The study of local animal life, especially the two-legged and sometimes violent vermin of which Finn was one.

Cacinnix held the theory, much mocked by other Vlantis, that those vermin had some primitive kind of intelligence. He even wondered if they might be descended – to a more animal level – from the beings who had built Earth's great civilization. Though of course that civilization had already been in ruins when the first Vlanti Controller and his Slavers (Cacinnix called them "Workers") had originally invaded Earth.

Cacinnix had pursued his theory, he went on, but had at first got nowhere – mostly because human captives tended to die or go mad at the sight of him. And also, the Vlantis had long ago decided that the human vermin should be *altered*, to erase whatever it was in their minds that made them react with aggression towards their alien rulers. So Cacinnix had to continue the cruel experiments that the Slavers conducted.

They had not had many successes, though at least they had bred the Bloodkin, who were useful. But now he had Finn, and he seemed to be on the threshold of proving his theory – that the human vermin *were* on a slightly higher level than other creatures of Earth.

"It may be," Cacinnix continued, "that you are a unique specimen, little Finn. You were born in the laboratories of the Workers. I need proof from others of your kind, as well. But still, you are a priceless breakthrough. What do you say to that, my little rat?"

Finn had been listening carefully to the idle flow of talk. He had even begun to relax slightly, to adjust to the idea of having met a towering, wrinkled, slime-wet monster who was one of the creators of the Slavers. But at the same time, what he had heard had continued to stir his anger.

"I say that you are evil and cruel," he replied, his voice harsh. "Ever since you and your creatures invaded this world, you have killed and tortured human beings. It would have been evil enough if you had thought we were just animals. But you say that *you* believe we are more than animals – and *still* you slaughter and enslave us." He was glaring at Cacinnix, his eyes blazing. "You are a monster, and you are blind and ignorant. Humans aren't animals, and they aren't vermin. We *can* talk, and think, and feel. And you could have found that out at any time, if you had looked at us properly, without all the killing and the cruelty."

Cacinnix seemed untroubled by the outburst. He turned away, poking a long finger at the machine.

"There is something wrong with this translator," he muttered. "You made many noises, little Finn, yet the machine gave out only broken fragments of words. It makes me wonder . . . Was that really speech? Or does my little rat merely make random noises which the *machine* makes me believe are speech?"

Finn snarled furiously. "It was speech, monster. But you probably wouldn't understand, anyway."

"On the other hand," Cacinnix went on, ignoring him, "little Finn might be speaking out of some strong *feelings*. The machine would find it impossible to translate primitive speech that contains strong feelings. I wonder – is my little rat overcome with fear, or hunger perhaps?"

Finn sank back, grinding his teeth with frustration. Despite the alien's theory about humans, despite what he had just learned about Finn, Cacinnix still felt that humans were not much more than beasts. So every one of his supposedly scientific studies of humanity was coloured by that prejudice. He could never accept or understand what humans really were. Especially if the translating machine was not as clever as it first seemed.

So, Finn realized, no matter what he said or did, Cacinnix would always see him and other humans as little rats. Little verminous creatures, to be captured, put to work, tormented, experimented on and casually killed, without a second thought.

The alien was turning away, still talking in that idle manner, as if to himself. But now the words were like ice-cold steel, stabbing into Finn.

"That will do for now," the alien was saying. "There are other duties to attend to before the night's rest. Tomorrow, I will spend the day with little Finn, make him speak some more, learn all that I can about him. And then perhaps I will cut him open, and see if he is formed differently from other rats."

Finn scarcely saw the towering being stalk out of the room. He huddled back in the energy cage, wild-eyed and sweating, as those last ominous words echoed in his mind. But then his gaze swung upwards, to the metal grating on the wall, where the strange device still hummed, pouring cold damp air into the room.

There was his way out of the Citadel, his escape from the giant alien's vicious plans. Yet he was still a rat in a trap, unable to move . . .

He started slightly as a door slid open. But it was not Cacinnix returning. A yellow-eyed Slaver marched into the room, taking up a position near the energy cage. A guard, Finn thought. The monster has sent one of his mechanical Workers to watch me, to be sure that I stay fit and well, to be cut open tomorrow.

Fit and well . . . The words thrust the seed of a thought into Finn's mind. Cacinnix would not want him harmed, until the alien's studies were complete . . .

For a moment he hesitated, fearful of what he was thinking. But it was the only chance he had. And if he could manage to get the timing right, it might just work.

He took a deep breath – and then, with a sudden jerk, he touched the back of his left hand against the energy cage.

Again the bolt of lightning flashed through him. Again his body convulsed, and his mouth gaped in that soundless scream.

The Slaver sprang forward, reaching frantically for the

switch that opened the cage. The lid slid back, and the clawed hands reached in, grasping Finn's jerkin, dragging him free of the shattering pain.

Finn's body wanted to sag with relief, wanted to lie back until the trembling faded and his heartbeat slowed. But he was filled with a desperate determination that ignored his body's wishes. Like a wild animal that can gnaw through its own leg to escape a trap, Finn's survival instinct overcame the pain.

Before the Slaver could withdraw, Finn's hands flashed upwards. They struck the alien's claws – slamming them sideways against the energy cage.

The Slaver stiffened, its body vibrating like a twig in a wind. Finn smelled a strange odour, like overheated metal as well as scorched flesh. The alien eyes darkened almost to black – and then all colour faded from them, and the Slaver crumpled.

Finn got to his feet, stepped carefully over the alien corpse and the cage's wall, then down to the floor. He felt dizzy and weak with the after-effects of the tension and shock. But he was out of the trap.

Out of one, anyway, he told himself.

He climbed up on another slab-table, beneath the metal grating. The cold air pouring in from the tunnel mouth made him shiver, but also cleared his head. He took hold of the grating, and jerked back with all his strength.

The metal did not move. Firmly fixed into the wall, it seemed that it would take an army to budge it.

Well, Finn thought, I wasn't going out of here alone, anyway.

He climbed down from the table, and glanced round. It was possible that Cacinnix might come back into the room, or send another Slaver, and find the cage empty. Then an alarm would be raised, and Finn's escape would be blocked.

Still, he felt he had a chance. The towering alien had said it was nearly time for his night's rest. And Finn had been in a Slaver centre at night. It had been as silent as an unoccupied tomb. The Bloodkin went to their own quarters at night and stayed there till morning. And Finn told himself firmly that all he had to do was to get out of the central sanctum, unseen. Out into the corridors. And then . . .

But he would think about that, if he stayed alive long enough to get that far.

Half-crouched, silent and alert as a hunting cat, Finn prowled towards the far door of the room.

PART THREE

The Last Battle

11
Out of the Sanctum

BAER CLAMBERED POWERFULLY up the steep, brush-covered slope, then halted on its crest, great chest swelling as he took in lungfuls of the clear air. Beyond that crest, he saw more slopes and ridges, each higher than the other like enormous, green-covered steps. Not too far beyond the last of those ridges, he knew, there was a long spur of bare rock, almost an escarpment. And beyond that . . .

He turned his head as the others came up behind him and also halted, staring around – at the slopes ahead, at the mighty mountain peaks whose rock-armoured shoulders loomed on every side.

"It's beautiful," Jena said quietly.

"Better'n deserts," Baer rumbled.

"Not to me," Rainshadow said firmly. "Nor to my people."

Baer gave him a half-grin. "Better'n the Firesands, then, anyway."

"I'll go along with that," Marakela said. "An' I reckon ol' Josh would, too."

But Josh was still back near the foot of the slope, moving more slowly now, his exhausted body no longer responding so readily to the urgings of his will. Baer had taken the lead, guiding the army through the mountains he knew so well.

It was the fifth day of their forced march. They had kept up their steady pace, travelling on into each night, starting again each morning well before dawn. And now – at almost exactly the same time that Finn was discovering the strange tunnel mouth in the thicket – Baer had brought them within half a day's march of their goal.

The foot of the long spur of rock, which was not yet visible behind the farthest ridge, led to the pass that would bring the warriors on to the plateau of the Citadel.

The long days and nights of almost non-stop travel – and the tensions and shocks of that first day and night, amid the horrors of the Firesands – had taken their toll. The horses needed to be rested more often, especially when they had to tackle the steep slopes of the uplands. And there were younger warriors who were no less weary and straggling than old Josh. So Rainshadow was halting the army more often, and for slightly longer rests. Yet even so they were on schedule.

Their plan – Baer's plan – was to reach the plateau in the depths of the night. Then the warriors could find cover on the plateau, rest awhile, and be ready and in position when the Bloodkin brought out the slaves in the morning.

So they paused again on that ridge-crest, chewing more strips of dried meat, drinking their fill from a nearby mountain spring. The sun was warm, and the light breeze was perfumed with the scent of flowers from a mountain meadow. And yet broad-shouldered Marakela shivered, as she stared out across the heights.

"I keep gettin' this feelin'," she said in a low voice. "Like, this is it, maybe for all of us. As if none of us are ever gonna leave the Citadel, alive."

"Many of us feel the same," Rainshadow said. "I have felt it for a long time. It may be that what we are planning to do at the Citadel will be impossible. But it is good that we will try. It is better to die here, fighting our last battle for the sake of our friend, than to be cut down by the Slaver whirlsleds."

Jena frowned as she looked at them. "I've never heard you talk this way before."

"Never felt this way before," Marakela said, with a gusty sigh. "Most times, goin' into a fight, I feel good – like nothin' can hurt me. But now . . . It's like somethin' cold touched me, an' said, Marakela, this's *it*."

Rainshadow nodded sombrely, and other warriors resting nearby murmured their quiet agreement.

"I ain't sayin' I don't wanta go on," Marakela added quickly. "I been a warrior all my life, an' I never figured on dyin' in bed of old age." She grinned. "I'm almost lookin' forward to it. If we get a chance t' have a crack at the Citadel, it'll be the best fight ever. An' that's a good way t' go."

"That is also true," Rainshadow said. "Especially now that it seems our free life on the Wasteland is finished."

Standing a short distance away from the group, Baer listened to their words, and looked at their darkly determined expressions. And a terrible sadness gripped him. All three hundred of those young, fearless people were ready to do battle against an impregnable fortress and a far larger force of Bloodkin – and were ready to die in that battle, for the sake of their friend Finn, and for the sake of striking one last glorious blow at the enemy.

Yet, Baer thought, these people shouldn't be talking of death. He looked at his friends – Rainshadow, calm and courageous; Marakela, with her fierce reckless grin; and Jena. Jena, who was as brave and fierce as any of them, yet who was still also a young and pretty girl – the girl for whom Finn and Baer had made their perilous trek across the land, so that she might live.

Not these, Baer thought. Especially not Jena. There's got to be another way.

And even as the thought formed in his mind, he was moving. With the skill that the months with Finn had taught him, he stepped silently backwards, away from the group, towards the shadowed depths of the brush around him. And not one of the warriors had even glanced his way when at last he was swallowed up by the foliage.

Several hours after the small Wasteland army had paused for that brief rest on the ridge-top, Finn also came temporarily to rest.

He had been through a time of sweaty, nerve-racked tension since he had first, hesitantly, opened the door that led out of Cacinnix's chamber. To his relief, the next connecting chamber had held no Slavers – just the array of strange machines and dimly glowing screens, now blank. But then he had crossed that room to another door, and had nearly wrecked his escape plan before it began.

Two Slavers were in the room ahead of him. They had their backs to the door, but were beginning to turn at the sound of the door opening.

Finn reacted with the instinctive reflex of a wild animal. His conscious mind had barely registered the two aliens when he was flinging himself, frantically but soundlessly, behind one of the heavy consoles of machinery that stood nearby. He crouched there, his heart thundering against his ribs, desperately wishing he had a weapon of some sort, and waited to be discovered.

He heard the Slavers speaking to each other in their gargling tones. Then he heard footsteps, as the two aliens stalked towards the door which – to them – had mysteriously opened by itself.

Finn slid away, keeping the bulk of the machine between himself and the Slavers as they strode by. The aliens stopped at the door, and exchanged a few more gargling noises. Then, to Finn's surprise, they turned around and strode back to resume what they had been doing.

He told himself that he should not be surprised. The Slavers were wholly without imagination, and so would never suspect that there could be anything threatening about the opening of the door. Perhaps they assumed it was a mechanical fault. Certainly they would never conceive of the chance that the human prisoner could have escaped from Cacinnix's lair.

So they had simply gone back to work. And Finn crouched uncomfortably behind that metal console, hardly daring to breathe, for nearly an hour – until at last the two aliens turned away, leaving the room by a different door.

Then Finn fled across the room like a man pursued by demons. Another door brought another moment of quivering tension – and then another, and another . . . But all the adjoining rooms were free of Slavers. Even the last room, the huge chamber with the gruesomely preserved corpses, contained no aliens.

And at last Finn was slipping through the broad, high doorway that led out of the secret sanctum, back into the main corridors of the third level.

It was deep night now, he knew, for he had a wild thing's inner sense of time. The Bloodkin would be in their quarters on the level below, well out of the way. And the few remaining Slavers would – he hoped – all be back in one or another of the rooms in that circular complex that was the sanctum. With luck, he would now have a clear run back down to the lowest level, and the slave chamber.

He was moving rapidly as those thoughts formed, drifting through the twisting passageways. But then the luck that he hoped for seemed to come to an end. Ahead, he heard footsteps – two sets, Slavers by the sound of them, on their way towards him along the same corridor. In a second, he knew, they would come around the angled corner ahead, and he would be spotted.

But he did not turn and flee. He ran *forward* – a few desperate sprinting strides, which brought him to a narrow door that opened off that corridor. Slapping the touch panel, he leaped through the door, and it slid shut behind him in the instant before the Slavers appeared.

And in that small narrow room, several dozen pairs of eyes were fixed on him, glaring and glinting.

He had gone rigid with panic when he first saw those eyes – but then he relaxed, sagging against the wall. The room was some kind of store-room, for a variety of small and peculiarly-shaped metal objects. And among those objects, arranged neatly on unsymmetrical shelves, were the glassy eyes – and *only* the eyes – that would normally be found in spywings.

Beyond the door he heard the two Slavers march past, not hesitating or slowing. And when their footsteps died away, he slid warily back out into the corridor, and continued on his way.

Moments later, a column of yellow light had wafted him down to the level below. There too he moved silently along the passages, listening to the snores of sleeping Bloodkin – and feeling that he might have marched along pounding a drum without disturbing any of those noisy sleepers. Then another of the strange elevators took him down to the lowest level.

Moving more swiftly, he hurried along the route that would bring him back to the slave chamber. And his tension eased slightly. He was safe now, for no Slavers would be down on the slave level of the Citadel. And he did not let himself think, yet, of how he was going to manage to get two dozen numbed and probably terror-maddened slaves back up through those levels, and into the sanctum.

All he knew was that, for their sake and especially for Steelfinder's, he was going to try.

He came to the door of the slave chamber, and paused. The corridor was empty, as far as he could see. But because it twisted around a sharp corner, ahead of him,, he relied more on his other senses. And they told him that all was silent, that nothing was moving, and that there were no unexpected odours. Just a slight scent of damp earth, the smell of muddiness – probably brought in by the slaves who had been working outside in the rain.

He reached forward to the touch-panel that would switch off the protective energy screen, and open the slave chamber door. As he did so, another icy flash of panic swept through him.

He had heard a faint shuffling noise, behind him.

He whirled, eyes wide and wild. And there, looming before him, forcewhip in hand, was a massive bulk of muscle covered in thick, coal-black hair, with a dark and matted beard hanging down in two strands, like a fork.

12
Flight of the Slaves

AGAIN FINN REACTED with the instincts of the wilds. He was still whirling when he bared his teeth in a snarl and changed the whirl into a leap – straight at the shaggy, black-furred throat. But just as swiftly, a huge hairy hand, damp and muddy, flashed up to slam against Finn's chest, driving him back against the wall.

And he stayed there, knees almost buckling with total surprise. Because the huge Bloodkin had spoken, in a deep, melodious bass.

"Finn, hold on!" Baer said. "It's me!"

Finn was finally able to focus his eyes and see past the black pelt and the forked beard, smeared and matted with wet mud that masked the familiar scent of his friend.

"What . . ." Finn stuttered. "How . . .?"

"How'd I get here?" Baer said, eyes twinkling. "That's what I was gonna ask *you*."

And when at last Finn could speak, the two friends stood in that alien corridor, grinning at each other with the sheer joy of reunion, and told each other what had been happening, and how they had come to be there at the same time.

They told their stories swiftly, in as few words as possible. Finn was filled with a soaring delight at the news of Josh, with dark sorrow at the news of the whirlsleds' final push against the warriors, and with awe at the account of the small army's hellish crossing of the Firesands. And finally Baer told him of their entry into the mountains, and how he had left the others, that very day.

"What they're plannin' could be plain suicide," he said. "An' I figured if I got here first, maybe they wouldn't hafta fight that 'last battle'. 'Cause I had an idea."

His idea required him to travel without stopping so as to reach the plateau before sundown. And he had just made it. He had moved unseen, through the grass and brush, to where a small party of slaves was being gathered together to be herded back inside for the night. It was a group with only one Bloodkin in charge – the one called Forkbeard.

"I know him," Finn said harshly.

"That figures," Baer rumbled. "I knew him too. He was one of them that nearly killed me, 'fore throwin' me outa the Citadel to die." The deep-set eyes glinted. "But now he's lyin' out there in a thicket, an' he won't beat anybody anymore."

Then, while the exhausted slaves stood numbly waiting, not even seeing what was happening, Baer had used handfuls of dark mud left by the rain to darken his pelt, and had separated his curly beard into two strands, like a fork. And at last he simply gathered up the slaves, and – with Forkbeard's forcewhip – had marched them into the Citadel.

"Ever'body's always busy gettin' slaves on their way down here, an' nobody looked at me twice," he said. "I sent my group of slaves to join another bunch an' I ducked down a side passage an' hid in a storeroom. After dark, when everythin' was quiet, I just snuck down here to find you."

"You found me," Finn said with a smile.

"I found a wild crittur goin' for my throat," Baer grumbled, with a crooked grin of his own. "But I'm kinda glad to see you, you crazy kid. You all right?"

"A few bruises, but they're healing," Finn said.

Then it was Finn's turn to explain how he had come to be creeping through the Citadel, miraculously outside the slave chamber. And it was Baer's turn to be awed and amazed – especially at the news of Cacinnix.

"That big crittur coulda been here when I was here," Baer said. "An' none of the Bloodkin ever knew!"

"I think he stays in the sanctum, with his machines and his 'studies'," Finn said sourly. "He doesn't seem to have much time for . . . lesser beings."

Baer tugged at his beard, now resuming its normal shape, and glanced at the slave chamber door. "An' you figure on gettin' these poor folks up there, to that sanctum, an' out through the tunnel?"

"It's the only way," Finn said. "With luck the corridors will be empty. And there aren't *that* many Slavers in the sanctum. We might make it." His lips twisted in a mirthless smile. "Unless the slaves are too afraid even to start moving."

Baer grinned, and the orange filament flickered out from the forcewhip in his hand. "You got nothin' to worry about. They'll move."

"Awright, worms, on yer feet!"

The rumbling roar echoed around the slave chamber. And the two dozen ragged humans began stumbling slowly up out of their sleep. They were even more numb and dazed than usual, after that abrupt awakening, but they had no way of knowing that it was still the middle of the night. All they knew was that a Bloodkin with a forcewhip was bellowing orders. Blindly, they obeyed.

But Steelfinder had sprung up, staring with astonishment at the fact that Finn had come into the room with the Bloodkin. And then her eyes widened further, as she recognized Baer through his disguise.

By then Finn had reached her. "We're getting out, Steelfinder," he said quickly. "I'll need your help, with these people."

She nodded, recovering her grave calm, as Baer roared again.

"Now listen, worms! You're gonna follow those two worms outa here." He pointed to Finn and Steelfinder, with a broad wink that only they saw. "An' I want you to go *quiet*. I mean *real* quiet. You don't let your feet make a sound on the floor. You don't even *breathe*, unless you can do it without a noise. Understand?" He took a step forward, the forcewhip flashing orange. "'Cause anyone makes the littlest, tiniest noise – he won't get a chance to make another. *Ever*!"

The frightened slaves cowered, and Baer glanced at Finn, his eyes showing his distaste for what he was doing. But Finn nodded reassuringly. He also hated having to terrify the wretched humans further, but it was the only way. Many might have been too dazed and crushed to understand if he had told them the truth. And those that did understand might have frozen with panic at the thought of what they were about to do.

So Finn and Steelfinder led the way, out into the empty, tomb-silent corridors.

And the Bloodkin menace of Baer, herding the slaves along, had the effect that was needed. The huddled group moved silently, not daring even to let a ragged shirtsleeve brush against dirt-caked trousers. And even Finn's hearing could barely detect the movements of the two dozen terrified humans who were following him.

They reached an elevator without incident, and went carefully up to the Bloodkin level. They crept just as noiselessly through those corridors, sweating with fright at the sound of raucous snoring from behind every doorway. Then another elevator brought them to the third level – and Finn halted the small cavalcade, to talk to Baer.

"I'm going to scout ahead," he whispered, "to make sure the way is clear." Swiftly he described the route that Baer would have to take to the broad outer door of the sanctum, and its hidden lock.

"I will come with you," Steelfinder said.

Finn shook his head. "I'll be all right alone."

"That's what you thought when you got into this mess," Baer pointed out.

"Maybe," Finn said, with a half-smile. "But you'll need Steelfinder to help with the slaves, inside the sanctum. There are things in there that could scare them to death."

"They're 'bout as scared now as they can get," Baer rumbled. "But we'll watch 'em. You watch your*self*."

Finn nodded, and moved swiftly away, into the mazy corridors.

Once again he drifted along between the dimly glowing metal walls, skin prickling with tension. But this time he met no wandering Slavers. The twisting passageways remained silent and empty, all the way to the sanctum's broad outer door. And, once he had found the secret lock and slipped back into those chambers of horrors, his luck held. Room after room seemed empty of Slavers.

Until he reached the second-last room, which held the twelve flickering screens that had briefly shown him pictures of the war on the Wasteland.

The screens were flickering again, but with a different picture. Each one of the glowing rectangles now held a close-up, moving image of the long, wrinkled, evilly ugly face of Cacinnix.

And the screens were being watched by eight Slavers, standing still and silent, their eyes a luminous orange-red as they watched and listened to their master.

By reflex, Finn drew back, looking for a hiding place. But, oddly, not one of the aliens turned towards him. It was as if they were rooted, riveted, by what they were seeing and hearing, so they had not noticed the opening of the door, partly behind them.

Finn stepped backwards out of the room, and let the door close, leaning against it, his heart hammering. They would have to find another way, through the encircling, interconnecting chambers, into the central lair of Cacinnix, where the tunnel was. He would have to go back and find Baer and the slaves, and re-direct them.

He began to retrace his steps. And as he went, an edge of curiosity made him wonder what it was that Cacinnix had been saying to the Slavers, on those screens. Without the translating machine, it had been nothing but alien gobbling sounds. But by the Slavers' rapt attention, it must have been important . . .

His musings ended, and thought fled from his mind. He had re-entered the outer chamber, where the grisly bodies of the dead humans and animals floated in the containers of liquid. And since he had passed through that room, four Slavers had entered it.

These aliens were not preoccupied with images on a screen. They turned and saw him before he could move. Eyes darkening to flaming crimson, they took up sharp-bladed implements from a slab-table nearby, and moved towards him.

Finn was unwilling to flee, for a pursuit might drive him back the way he came, back to the inner room where the eight Slavers were watching the screens. So he circled, crouching and wary, like a panther facing a pack of wolves.

The Slavers seemed unhurried, as if they knew that he had no hope of escaping them. Slowly they advanced, the blades glinting. And just as Finn was wondering if he might gain an advantage by a surprise attack, another inner door of the room slid open. And he went cold with the knowledge that he had no chance now at all.

Eight more Slavers had entered the room – perhaps, Finn thought dully, the ones who had been watching the screens. They were unarmed, but even so there were too many of them, and their three-clawed hands would be dangerous enough.

He backed away, until his retreat was halted by the chill side of one of the ghastly containers. And he waited, and watched, for the attack that would finish him.

But, instead, he heard the sound of yet another door opening. The broad, heavy outer door of the sanctum. Finn did not even turn his head, expecting more Slavers. But the twelve aliens turned – and their eyes darkened to an evil purple, just as Finn heard the amazing sound.

A hissing intake of breath – in a human mouth.

Then he turned to look. Steelfinder was standing in the doorway, her face blank and cold, staring at the group of aliens – unmoving, as five of the twelve began to stalk towards her.

Finn would have called to her to run, but he did not have the chance. And, he learned, she would not have fled, anyway. She was a Wasteland warrior – and, Finn then discovered, a prodigious one.

As the five Slavers moved nearer, Steelfinder took two light running steps – *towards* them. Then she leaped, high in the air, one leg flashing forward. The kick nearly tore a Slaver's head from its neck. And even as she landed, her hands were slashing like blurred axe-blades, and two more aliens toppled, their own necks oddly bent.

The remaining two of the five reached out with clawed hands, but clutched only empty air. Steelfinder slid gracefully under the claws, and struck again – another axe-blow, another high sweeping kick. And suddenly, in what could not have been more than four seconds from entering the room, she was standing alone among five alien corpses.

And by then Finn was moving. He ducked low, and slid backwards underneath the slab-table holding the container that had been behind him. The four Slavers nearest to him turned back to face him. But they were too late.

Finn had already begun to surge up, under the container, with all the strength in his compact body. The table tipped forward, and the huge container went with it – crashing forward and down, directly on top of the bunched group of Slavers.

The room was filled with the echoing thunder of the container's fall, the huge splash of liquid, the brief gargling cries of the aliens – which were cut off at once. All four had been caught beneath that crushing weight, and only one of them was still wriggling feebly.

By then Steelfinder was moving purposefully towards the remaining three Slavers. They were backing away, their eyes almost black. But they did not take more than two steps. A bright glitter of metal curved through the air – a spinning blade hurled with lethal accuracy by a powerful, immensely skilled hand. The machete sliced through two spindly alien necks, just as Steelfinder leaped again, with another flashing kick.

And then there were no more Slavers alive in the room.

"Thought you weren't gonna leave me any," Baer growled, lumbering through the door.

"Where are the slaves?" Finn asked anxiously.

"Just outside," Baer said. "They won't go anywhere. But I heard the racket, and thought I'd better check." He stared around, eyes grim. "If this is the sanctum, I'm glad I never got in before."

Finn turned to Steelfinder, and found her staring with a frozen expression at the floor. And Finn himself turned pale. The container that he had tipped over on to the aliens had been the one that held the body of Keller.

"I'm sorry," Finn whispered numbly.

Steelfinder nodded grimly. "Keller will not mind. He would be glad to know that even in death he could strike back at them."

Baer shifted restlessly. "Let's get movin'. There could be more Slavers comin' along."

"And Bloodkin," Steelfinder said, "if an alarm has been raised."

"Nope," Baer said with a grim smile. "Not in here. Slavers wouldn't let Bloodkin into the sanctum even to get us."

"Good," Finn said, his own smile echoing Baer's. "Then you two get the slaves, and I'll go on ahead again. There were Slavers in a room farther on – but these may be the same ones."

And so it proved. When he reached the room with the twelve

screens, it was deserted. And the screens also were blank now – so Cacinnix's mysterious message had been delivered.

He crept forward finally to the door that led to his goal – the lair of the giant alien, where the tunnel was, offering freedom. For a moment he paused, wondering if the noise of the fight could have penetrated this far. But then he took a deep breath, knowing that there was only one way to find out, and pressed the touch-panel to open the door.

The cold, damp air of Cacinnix's room poured out around him. And Finn stood rooted.

From in front of the larger screen that was embedded in the opposite wall, Cacinnix turned toweringly towards him. The great eyes were glowing a malevolent purple – and the long slender tube of a heatlance was held, almost casually, in one vast hand.

13
The Message

THE LIPLESS MOUTH opened, and the gobbling sounds emerged. And to Finn's surprise the translating machine was still switched on.

"Clever little rat," Cacinnix said through the machine. "Able to kill a Worker and escape the cage. But not clever enough to escape the sanctum. How long has my rat been wandering from room to room – so hopelessly lost that he has come full circle back to where he started?"

Though fear was squeezing Finn's throat, he stood calmly, studying the giant alien. He knew he could not turn and run. With Baer and the slaves coming along soon, Cacinnix had to be got out of the way – at any cost. And at least, if the monster believed that Finn was a lost and terrified beast, he would not summon Slavers to his aid.

Cacinnix's next words confirmed that hope. "Now that the little rat is so terrified he cannot move," the alien voice went on, still as if he were talking idly to himself, "I could get him back into his cage without trouble. But there is no point. I have no more need of little rats, in cages or not."

That remark puzzled Finn. And the next one was even more mystifying.

"Did you see the message on the screens, little Finn, in the room beyond?" Cacinnix asked. "But you would not have understood. You would not understand now, if I replay the transmission. But I will replay it. Then we can again see the face of Ikkarok, and hear his message. Ignorant, narrow-minded Ikkarok, who has no time for science, for the gathering of knowledge." He gestured with the heatlance. "Come closer, Finn, and see the stupidity of Ikkarok."

The towering alien reached back and adjusted some controls below the huge screen. And Finn slowly edged forward, keeping a wary eye on the heatlance. He understood little of what Cacinnix was saying. But he had grasped the idea that the alien he had seen on the Slavers' twelve screens had *not* been Cacinnix, but another monster called Ikkarok. And the anger in Cacinnix's voice was aimed not at Finn but at whatever the other alien had said, in his "message".

Then the face of the other alien appeared on the large screen, and Finn could now see the slight difference between it and the face of Cacinnix, when they were side by side. He also dimly understood – though he knew nothing of recordings – that Cacinnix was somehow causing the screen to show Ikkarok's message again.

The machine spoke, and the words of Ikkarok reached Finn's ears. And as he listened, Finn began to react. He began to look as if he had suddenly come face to face with the most hideous evil in the universe. And as if that monstrousness was destroying his mind.

He turned stark white. His teeth clenched fiercely, his lips twitching back from them. Every cord of his neck stood out with a frenzied tension. His hands trembled slightly, and cold sweat beaded his forehead. And his unblinking eyes stared at the screen as if at the mouth of an inferno.

Steadily, the voice of the alien called Ikkarok droned on from the machine. And Finn stood immobile, unaware of anything except the overwhelming assault of those words.

Then the message, the recording, came to an end, and Ikkarok's face vanished from the screen. Finn might have gone on standing there, in that frozen, deathly trance. But he had been listening to the translator machine – and when Cacinnix spoke, through the machine, Finn heard those words too.

"If you could understand, little rat," the alien said, "you would know why I am angry at ignorant Ikkarok. I am forbidden to continue my studies of yourself and other rats. I must bring them to an end. And I think it best, little Finn, to begin by bringing *you* to an end."

As he spoke, moving unhurriedly, he raised the heatlance and levelled it at Finn's face.

Finn was still standing as before – pale, rigid, blank-eyed. His conscious mind seemed to have fled into some deep cavern within himself, in the face of the shattering impact of the words he had heard from the screen. But his conscious mind was not required, at that instant. As Cacinnix took aim, Finn reacted by sheer instinct – the instinct of a wild creature, when its life is threatened, no matter how large or fearsome its enemy is.

With a growl like a maddened wolf, Finn sprang at the alien.

Taken totally by surprise, Cacinnix flinched away from the furious attack. His hand jerked, and the heat-beam sliced redly through the air, missing Finn by half a metre. And then Finn struck upwards, fists lashing at the vast, wrinkled body looming above him.

His blows might have had little effect on all that sagging, slime-wet flesh. But one furious fist struck Cacinnix's long forearm, and jolted the heatlance from his hand.

Then Cacinnix struck out, with his other hand, to ward Finn off. It was an awkward, open-handed blow, but it slammed against Finn with awesome weight, flinging him halfway across the room. He crashed against one of the slab-tables, and found his feet by bracing himself with one hand on the table-top. The fingers of that hand touched something cold and metallic – and a wild-eyed glance showed that it was a slim, sharp-bladed instrument. Perhaps it was what Cacinnix might have used to dissect Finn, but the thought did not enter his blindly maddened mind.

He snatched it up, and as the monster stooped to reclaim the heatlance, Finn sprang again.

Cacinnix kicked out furiously to keep Finn away, and Finn struck. The glittering blade sliced deeply into the baggy folds of skin in the giant's leg. Yellowish blood gushed – but Cacinnix seemed hardly to notice the wound. His huge three-fingered hand lashed out again, in another thundering blow.

Finn fell, rolled and came swiftly to his feet, blade ready, bracing himself against the edge of another of the metal slab-tables. Cacinnix loomed above him, lunging down with huge hands ready to grasp and crush. At the last instant, Finn dodged under those reaching hands, stabbing again with the blade at the giant's injured leg. Once again Cacinnix did not seem to react to the wound. But the blade had done some damage, and the injured leg crumpled beneath the giant's weight. Cacinnix lurched forward, off balance, beginning to fall.

And, trying to break his fall, his huge hands slammed down like clubs on top of the gleaming energy cage that still rested on the slab-table behind Finn.

The cage collapsed with a muffled, explosive crash. But the deadly energies remained intact. With a small strange noise like a whimper, Cacinnix stiffened and convulsed. His huge wrinkled body shuddered in ghastly spasms. And then he crumpled to the floor, the scorched hands pulling free from the shattered cage.

For a long moment Finn stood perfectly still. His blade was still held ready, he was still poised in a fighting crouch, as if he did not realize that the unequal combat was over. Then, as if every muscle was stiff and painful, he slowly straightened. The blade fell unheeded from his limp hand. The survival instinct that had driven him to fight for his life was no longer needed. He became, once again, the white-faced, empty-eyed zombie whose mind seemed to have given way under some unbearable shock.

He stumbled backwards, not even glancing at the fallen alien.

When his back met the far wall, he simply slid downwards, till he was sitting motionlessly on the floor, staring into nothingness.

He was still sitting in the same position when the far door of the chamber slid open.

Baer came through the door in a rush, machete in his hand, looking tense and grim as if expecting the worst. But when he saw Finn sitting unharmed, he relaxed.

"Got worried, waitin' for you to come back," he said, as he slid the machete into its sheath. "What's been . . ."

His voice faded as he caught sight of the giant body of Cacinnix, sprawled on the floor half-under the slab-table.

"Dam'!" Baer breathed. "So that's the crittur? Glad I never ran into it when I was a kid in the Citadel. Woulda scared me outa ten years' growth. What'd you do to it?"

Finn said nothing. He had not moved since Baer had entered the room. He merely stared straight ahead, lost in his private nightmare.

"Finn?" Baer finally realized that something was very wrong. "You hurt? What is it?"

The resonant bass voice seemed to penetrate some of the cloud around Finn's shocked mind. Slowly he moved his empty gaze towards Baer.

"All over," he said, in a hollow croak that was nothing like his own voice. "It's all over."

Baer took a step forward, worriedly. But a sudden commotion at the door distracted him. The group of humans was coming in, with Steelfinder.

The slaves no longer needed the threat of Baer's presence to stay huddled, coweringly, together. The sights they had seen coming through the sanctum had driven most of them to the edge of hysteria – or even deeper into a blank-eyed daze that resembled Finn's. And the sight of the monstrous form of Cacinnix, on the floor, pushed the hysterical ones over the edge.

Several of them screamed. Three of them fainted. The others whimpered and trembled, eyes wild and bulging, as if they were about to break into frenzied, mindless flight. It took several minutes before the combination of Baer's menace and Steelfinder's soothing calm could restore something like order, and quiet.

Then Steelfinder and Baer went back to Finn.

"He does not seem injured," Steelfinder said, frowning anxiously.

"Seems not," Baer agreed. "I saw him like this once before, when he had a bad shock. This big crittur musta given him a rough time."

He reached down to shake Finn gently. "Finn, it's me. C'mon now – say somethin'."

Again Finn's empty eyes moved slowly towards Baer. "It's . . . all over," he said, as before, in the same hollow voice.

Baer shook his head, then glanced round. "Keep an eye on him," he told Steelfinder. "I gotta get these folks movin' 'fore we're trapped in here. All this creepin' round the corridors an' stuff has used up mosta the night."

He looked up at the grating across the ventilation tunnel, which was just as Finn had described it to him. Clambering up on a slab-table, he gripped the grating, and heaved. The mighty muscles of his back bunched and rolled like boulders. And the solidly fixed metal peeled away from the wall as if it had been strips of cloth.

Just behind the grating, the strange machine still hummed, pouring the cold, damp air into the room. But Baer's great hands wrenched it loose just as easily, with a shriek of torn metal. The humming stopped, the cold blast of air died away.

Baer dropped the broken machine, and glanced around. Finn was still silent and blank as a wax figure. And the slaves still huddled, many of them weeping quietly.

"Back in a second," Baer said to Steelfinder. He heaved himself up, pushing his great shoulders into the mouth of the tunnel, and then – threshing and wriggling – vanished from sight.

The slaves nearly went hysterical again at the sounds that followed – two hollow, echoing booms, as Baer smashed his way unstoppably through the second grating, at the tunnel's other end.

A moment later, he reappeared, sliding back out of the tunnel with a grunt. "All clear," he told Steelfinder. "You go first, an' I'll push these folks along after you." He gave her a crooked half-grin. "Look out for company. There oughta be about three hunnerd warriors up there on the plateau, comin' to find out what all that racket was about."

Steelfinder's eyes lit up. Lithely, she sprang to the tunnel. Then, one at a time, with threats and angry growls, Baer drove the weeping, shivering, panicky humans into the tunnel mouth, and sent them on their way to the one thing they least expected – freedom.

When the last one had finally climbed out of sight, Baer threw the forcewhip aside with some relief, and turned back to Finn.

"It worked, Finn," he rumbled, "just like you figured. Now we gotta get goin', too. It's gonna be dawn out there, real soon."

He reached down, carefully pulling Finn to his feet. Finn did not resist, but merely stood there. His eyes had not changed, nor his voice, nor the words spoken in that voice. "It's all over," he said once more.

Baer frowned, feeling chilled by some unknown fear. "What's all over? The war on the Wasteland?" He peered into Finn's empty eyes. "Seems you found out somethin' pretty bad, son. What is it?"

Something stirred vaguely in the back of Finn's eyes – as if his mind was fighting to regain control of his shocked and numbed being. But if he was going to speak again, he did not have the chance.

Baer heard a sudden shuffling thump behind him. He whirled

– and total horror made him grunt, as if he had been kicked in the stomach.

Cacinnix was rising to his feet.

Yellow blood still seeped from the wounds caused by Finn's blade. But the monster towered up to his full four-metre height, his eyes glittering a murderous icy purple – and his vast hands, despite being seared by the energy cage, were clenched into fists like giant menacing clubs.

14
Spacefleet

"SO THE LITTLE rat has a hairy helper."

Baer twitched with surprise, hearing the gobbling sounds from Cacinnix's mouth, and then the words in the language of Earth from the nearby machine. But despite his surprise, his hand had moved in a blur to draw the glinting machete.

"The rat tried to fight, and now the hairy one will try," Cacinnix snarled. "Foolish creatures. Pain is merely a brief discomfort to me. The bites of verminous creatures cannot seriously damage a Vlanti."

He took a step forward. And Baer, a savage growl rumbling in his throat, flexed his powerful forearm and hurled the machete, with all of his matchless skill. The razor-edged blade flashed across the narrow space, and buried itself for half its length in the giant alien's chest.

Cacinnix staggered, with a grating noise like a strangled cough. But then again he straightened, almost casually plucking the machete from his chest and flinging it aside. He paid no attention to the new stream of yellow blood gushing from the wound. And then he lunged forward, and one massive fist crashed into Baer's chest.

It was like a blow from a battering-ram. Baer's great bulk was hurled backwards, to crash heavily into the far wall. But the big Bloodkin recovered at once from the bruising impact. Roaring with rage, he launched himself into a bare-handed attack on the giant.

Again Cacinnix swung an enormous fist, in a backhanded blow that swept Baer off his feet, and flung him sideways – where his head hit the side of a slab-table with a meaty thump. For a moment Baer was stunned, unable to make his limbs move. And in that moment, Cacinnix turned to Finn.

Finn was rigid as a statue, even more white-faced and wide-eyed at the new shock of the alien's apparent return to life. The giant hands closed around his body before he could move, and lifted him from his feet. Instinctively, desperately, Finn struggled, striking and kicking at the mighty fingers that gripped him. But Cacinnix did not seem to notice the blows. His eyes were almost a demonic black as he tightened his grip.

Finn cried out as the monstrous pressure bore down on his ribs. A dark film seemed to be veiling his eyes, and his struggles grew weaker. He was not aware of Baer staggering forward, still half-stunned but trying to come to his aid – only to be flung away again by an almost contemptuous kick from Cacinnix.

And then, for Finn, came the most unexpected shock of all.

The crushing, grinding grip suddenly began to ease, to relax. The terrible hands of Cacinnix slowly opened, letting Finn fall in a heap to the floor. And those hands reached up to the wrinkled folds of flesh at the monster's throat, scrabbling at the skin.

"No . . ." the alien voice said. The gobbling noise was nearly a whispering croak. "No ... Too hot ... dry ... cannot breathe . . . ."

The great head swung, and the purple-black eyes fixed on to the gaping hole where the grating on the ventilation tunnel had been.

"*No!*" Cacinnix croaked again, fear and fury in his gobbling voice. Twitching, staggering, the alien raised one vast foot, to bring it crushingly down on Finn, where he lay dazed and gasping.

But that final, vengeful attack was not completed. The monster tried to cry out, but the sound was only a grating, wheezing rasp. And then Cacinnix swayed, and stumbled – and toppled backwards like a felled tree.

For a moment more, the huge hands scrabbled feebly at the wrinkled throat. But then they fell away, limp and lifeless. And the deep purple-black of the eyes faded, until finally they were as blank and colourless as glass.

Baer moved painfully and warily forward, finding his machete, then peering down at the giant corpse. "Choked to death," he said wonderingly. "Sure musta needed that cold wet air."

Behind him Finn groaned as he tried to get up, his bruised ribs complaining. And Baer turned and unceremoniously hoisted him to his feet.

"C'mon," he said roughly. "It's gotta be dawn by now. Out we go – you first."

The final battle seemed to have stirred Finn partly out of the empty-eyed mindlessness that had frozen him before. He blinked at Baer, awareness returning to his eyes. And with it came an expression that contained misery, and anguish, and an infinity of despair.

"Baer –" he began.

"Yeah, I know," Baer growled. "It's all over – whatever it is. Just get goin', an' talk later."

He thrust Finn firmly towards the dark gape of the tunnel mouth. Then he glanced round, as if to be sure that Cacinnix was not about to rise once more from the dead. And finally he clambered up into the tunnel after Finn – to leave the Citadel for the last time.

Outside, the grass and brush of the plateau were just beginning to be visible, as the eastern sky became streaked with the first grey light of dawn. Steelfinder and the other slaves were standing a few paces outside the thicket that held the tunnel mouth. They were still in their terrified huddle, most of them dazed and stupefied, or weeping and trembling. But a few were beginning to stare around, something like wild hope kindling in their eyes.

Because, from the grass and brush all around them, humans had appeared. Humans with spears and bows, humans with fierce eyes but wide welcoming smiles. The three hundred Wasteland warriors had reached the Citadel.

As Baer and Finn emerged from the tunnel, and moved out of the thicket, they saw the small knot of people waiting, a few metres away. Finn's still dazed eyes slid across the amazed and delighted faces of Rainshadow and Marakela and Jena, then stopped when they took in the lean face of the old man next to Jena.

He took an unbelieving step forward. Then old Josh reached him, stretching out his hands, unable to speak, merely gripping Finn's shoulders. And Finn bowed his head, slowly, and began to weep.

They were dry, rasping sobs that seemed to shake his body like an autumn leaf rattling in a storm. The others looked stricken, stepping forward. But Jena reached him first, putting her arms around the two of them, father and foster brother.

"Finn, don't . . ." she began.

Then her soft tones were lost, by two sudden eruptions of nerve-rending sound.

The first was a high, drawn-out scream, from the throat of one of the freed slaves. It was almost an animal howl – the sound that is made when someone who thought he had escaped one horror finds himself facing another, even more monstrous.

And the second sound was a hissing, sweeping, rushing noise that all the humans knew only too well.

On to the far edge of the plateau, from the narrow pass that opened through the mountains, came hundreds of huge, hovering, metal egg-shapes. The Slaver whirlsleds had returned from the Wasteland.

Two by two, in a steady, unhurried stream, the menacing machines slid into view. And Rainshadow was the first of the humans to come to himself, from that final, soul-crushing despair.

"We must retreat!" he said urgently. "We can hide from them in the mountains!"

"No way," Baer said bleakly, gesturing at the rocky slopes around them that held the plateau like a cup. "They're blockin' the only way off the plateau. We'd have to climb the rock – an' they'd pick us off like bugs on a wall."

"Then this is it, like I figured," Marakela said, her jaw set hard, her eyes grim. "We stand an' fight. The last battle."

"There's no point," said a dull, flat voice behind her.

It was Finn who had spoken. He and his family had moved apart when the whirlsleds had appeared, to stare desolately at the sudden shattering of their hopes. Except that Finn did not seem to be looking at the Slavers. He seemed to be gazing, as before, at some unknown evil that only he could see.

"No point in anything," he went on, in that same empty voice. "It's all over."

"He keeps sayin' that," Baer growled. "Somethin' happened to him in the Citadel – wish I knew what."

"He's right enough, though," Marakela said darkly, her gaze fixed on the whirlsleds, still moving unhurriedly on to the far edge of the plateau. "It's sure all over – fer us, anyway."

"Finn – son," old Josh said, gripping Finn's arm with concern. "What . . ."

But then, as with Jena, his voice was drowned by a cataract of sound. It was a monstrous, thunderous blast, like the sudden roaring of a thousand maddened beasts. Everyone started and flinched, looking at the whirlsleds, in the chill certainty that they were accelerating into their final, sweeping, murderous charge.

But in fact the machines seemed to be slowing down, settling closer to the ground as their speed dropped.

And then, as the monstrous thunder battered at their hearing, the warriors looked up.

Some of them gasped and cried out. Some dropped to their

knees, as if their legs would no longer support them. Weapons fell from suddenly nerveless hands. And the light of battle faded from all their eyes, even Marakela's, as they looked at their certain, unavoidable destruction.

Silhouetted against the pearl-grey of the dawn sky was a host of immense, oddly-angled metal shapes. They were settling down slowly through the thin cloud cover, great jets of flame thundering beneath them. Many hundreds of them, growing more huge as they approached the earth – so that the watching humans realized that each of the machines was nearly twice as large as the Citadel itself.

The Slaver spacefleet – appearing as it must have appeared in the skies over Earth on the first day of their invasion, centuries before, while humans stared up in helpless, agonized horror.

As the warriors watched, frozen by that cataclysmic arrival, the host of mighty machines began to move apart. New thunder struck painfully down as they hurtled away, skimming the mountain-tops, heading in every direction of the compass. But two of the terrible ships continued their downward descent, towards the breadth of level ground on the north side of the Citadel.

In moments, the two immense shapes were settling, rock and earth spewing up from the flaming downward blasts. Then the ear-shattering bellow of the vast engines began to fade – and soon silence returned to the plateau. An ominous silence, in which the two ships loomed like newly-formed mountain peaks made of metal – their enormity dwarfing the smaller ship that had been flown by Cacinnix.

But then that silence in turn was broken. The plateau was again filled with a rushing, hissing hum, rising into a throbbing rumble. The Slaver whirlsleds had lifted higher from the ground, and were surging forward across the plateau.

Of all the humans watching certain death hurtling towards them, only Baer had the strength to move or speak. He grasped Finn's shoulder and shook him, half-lifting him from the ground.

"Is this what you meant?" he roared, his voice rough with rage and hopelessness. "The spaceships, comin' to wipe out humanity? To finish us off? Is *this* why you say it's all over?"

It was the question that every human on the plateau had silently asked, as they had watched that fleet of monstrous ships hurtle away in every direction, to countless other places around the world. The answer, from the advancing whirlsleds as well as the spaceships, was shatteringly obvious.

But then, to the total and overwhelming astonishment of everyone, Finn began to laugh.

It was wild laughter, but not mindless or insane. Everything that had happened since the death of Cacinnix seemed to be bringing him out of that frozen daze, where he had seemed like one whose mind had been broken by an ultimate horror. He looked like himself again, despite the wildness and the pain that could be heard in his laughter.

"*No!*" Finn yelled, almost savagely. "That's not it! They don't *care* about us any more! The ships are here to pick up the Slavers! Do you understand? *The Slavers are leaving Earth!*"

15
To Reclaim a World

THOSE FINAL FIVE words struck the others like an exploding bomb. All of them, including Baer, were stunned into an unbelieving silence.

And then they were stunned almost into mindlessness as they watched the deadly, onrushing whirlsleds simply speed past them, neither slowing nor changing direction, as if the three hundred and more humans on the plateau had suddenly become invisible.

They could not understand it, they could not accept it, they did not dare let themselves believe it. They simply stood, in the open, dazed and numb, much as Finn had stood in front of the huge screen in Cacinnix's lair. And they watched, blankly, as the Citadel erupted into high-speed activity.

If the alien structure had resembled an ants' nest, it now resembled such a nest that had been disturbed. The great entrance had opened as the whirlsleds drew near. And then the host of Slavers left their machines, and streamed into the Citadel. Shortly, they began to stream out again, with an enormous array of objects – mostly carried on hovering discs like the one that had supported Finn's energy cage.

By then vast cavernous doors had opened in the sides of the immense spaceships, and broad ramps had slid down to the ground. Back and forth the tireless streams of Slavers went, carrying all the contents of the Citadel – machinery, equipment of every sort, weapons – and stowing them on to the ships.

All through that long day the humans watched in numbed silence as the Slavers laboured steadily on. The Bloodkin, too, were pressed into service, and seemed – from their stumbling walk and bowed heads – to be as shocked and stunned as the watching humans. Not once, all that day, did a Slaver or a Bloodkin even glance towards the humans, standing openly on the plateau. The Slavers worked like the machines they partly were – and, by the time the afternoon shadows were beginning to lengthen, their enormous task was done.

The Slavers wasted no time on ceremony. The Citadel was now a stripped and empty shell, and the aliens did not give it a backward glance. They ignored the Bloodkin, standing in a milling crowd looking anxious and lost. At the end, when they carried out the huge limp form of Cacinnix, they treated even it as if it were another piece of equipment. Then, finally, the Slavers re-entered their whirlsleds. Two by two, the machines swept up the ramps and into the ships. The ramps withdrew, the vast doors slid shut.

And once again the plateau echoed with the titanic thunder of the spaceships' engines. The two metal immensities rose from the ground – gathering speed, dwindling in size as they gained height. At last they were two small glittering specks in the sky, like splashes of orange, as the setting sun reached up to touch them with its fiery glow.

An eye-blink later, they were gone. And the sky above the mountain peaks was clear and calm and empty, as if such a thing as alien spacecraft had never existed.

As darkness stole over the plateau, the humans slowly stirred themselves, and moved – stiffly, wearily, like people recovering from a long illness – to find their horses, and to begin the long ride out of the empty mountains, back to the Wasteland.

But that first night they rode only far enough to be well away from the Citadel when they made camp. And in that camp, the entire small army had clustered around Finn. They all could see that he was himself again – weary and drawn, but recovered from the shock of that inconceivable departure. And they needed him to talk to them, to tell them why and how the impossible had happened, so that they too could recover.

So Finn told them, with help from Baer and Steelfinder. About the weird conversations with Cacinnix, and about the nerve-twisting hours of the escape through the Citadel. And especially, they heard from Finn about the monstrous alien called Ikkarok, on that screen in Cacinnix's lair, and the message that had nearly wrecked Finn's mind.

"Ikkarok was superior to Cacinnix, in some way," Finn said. "And he wasn't pleased with Cacinnix. He said that the whole operation here was costing too much, and they weren't getting the *profit* they needed – from the metals and so on that the Slavers mined."

Baer snorted. "That figures. They been diggin' here for hunnerds of years. Couldn't last forever."

"But not only that," Finn said. "Ikkarok complained that they were losing too many Slavers and too much equipment. Because of the 'local vermin'."

"That's us!" Marakela said, with a fierce grin.

Finn nodded. "And Ikkarok said that it was Cacinnix's fault, because he was too busy *studying* the vermin, rather than dealing with them. Us."

Rainshadow frowned. "I do not understand. Why then did they not go on *dealing* with us? They came on to the Wasteland to exterminate us. Why did they not finish the job?"

"They would have," Finn said sombrely. "But Ikkarok's main message was that there was no longer any need to bother about us. Because another world had been discovered, a much 'richer', more profitable place. So they were shifting the whole operation, all the Slavers and everything, to that other world."

Jena shivered. "So whatever kind of beings live on that world, it's their turn now."

"No," Finn said,. "That was another good thing about the other world, Ikkarok said – no vermin."

"So they just upped an' left," Baer said heavily. "Not a Slaver on Earth any more. It's gonna be a time before I really believe that."

"I still can't believe those whirlsleds," Jena said, "going past us like we weren't there."

"That's what happened to me," Finn said in a low voice. "I couldn't take it in. I kept thinking about all the battles we've fought, all the warriors who've been killed . . . and it all seemed so *pointless*. When all we needed to do was just *wait* – and the Slavers would simply have gone away, because the Earth wasn't *profitable* any more!"

There was a long silence as the others savoured the bitterness of those words. But then Marakela shook her red head firmly.

"I c'n see how you woulda been hit hard, Finn," she growled. "But y're wrong. Even if we'd just waited, an' never fought back, people woulda still died. Mostly as slaves. We hadta fight."

"And you said yourself," Jena put in, "that one reason why they went away was because they were losing too much, because of us *vermin*."

"That is so," Rainshadow agreed. "Our fighting and dying were not pointless. And, Finn, it would not have been pointless even if it had *not* helped to drive the Slavers away." He leaned forward, dark eyes intent. "The human race will start to recover now, from the centuries of terror. It will take a long time – but in the end, human beings will reclaim their world. And they will be able to do so with *pride*. They will know that some humans fought the Slavers, and were ready to fight them still, on the last day, to the death. Humans will know that they were not merely *given* their world back, with contempt, by aliens who had no more use for it. They will know that, in a small way, some humans fought for their world, their freedom – and *won* it back!"

"That's true," Josh said. "If I know folks, they'll make the

Wasteland warriors inta legends. An' they'll be tellin' those stories with pride, hunnerds of years from now."

Baer grunted sourly. "Maybe they'll be too busy buildin' their civilization again, an' makin' new bombs to blow the world up with, like before."

"Perhaps not," Rainshadow said quietly. "Perhaps humans will never forget the centuries of their slavery, and the lessons that must be learned. They may never forget that they have to live together in peace and harmony – and use their power wisely – and care for their world properly."

"Or else," Marakela said fiercely, "some other buncha aliens could come an' take it away from 'em again."

The following days, the small army rode on its way eastwards. Reaching the foothills, they searched for and found the rest of the Wasteland people, where they had hidden after fleeing through the Firesands. And eventually, when all the people had finally grasped the unbelievable news that there were no more Slavers on Earth, the entire population of the Wasteland returned to their desert home – to begin a colossal celebration, lasting for days, and held in the open with no fear of lurking whirlsleds, or batwings in the sky.

During that time Finn and Josh and Jena hardly left one another. For them, in a special way, it was truly *all over*, as Finn had numbly repeated in the Citadel. They were re-united, in just the way that Finn had dreamed about, ever since the first days of his relentless quest across the continent. The impossible dream had come true – as had an even more impossible dream, with the departure of the alien invaders.

And Finn's closest friends also seldom strayed far from the three Ferrals, during that time of merry-making. Baer, of course, and Rainshadow and Marakela. And Steelfinder, who would still now and then glance at Finn as if waiting for him to perform some new miracle. Scar-faced Gratton joined them, his damaged leg healing, relishing his warm acceptance by the Wasteland people. And Corwin, full of curiosity about the Citadel and Cacinnix, looking as if he regretted not being able to have a talk himself with the giant alien.

But eventually the celebration came to an end. And with it came a time of quiet sadness, as the Wasteland people began to drift away.

Many of the warriors wanted to roam out across more of the western wilderness, to savour their freedom – and to carry the news of freedom to isolated human villages along the way. Corwin intended to join those wanderers, and so he was the first of Finn's closest friends to leave. And with him, Gratton came to say goodbye – for he was joining some others who were going to seek more fertile ground, and build the kind of peaceful and productive villages they had always dreamed of. Most of the desert Indians, including Steelfinder, intended to explore the Wasteland that was their home, to see how much of its tough and durable life had survived the Slaver whirlsleds. And so Finn had that further miserable parting, from the calm Indian woman who had been so important to him in the Citadel.

But there were some among the warriors who seemed restless and at a loss – including Marakela.

"I got too used t' the fightin'," the big redhead finally confessed. "Dunno what t' do. Can't just settle down, an' wait around t' be an old lady."

"There may still be fighting," Rainshadow said. "Every Slaver base in the land still has its Bloodkin."

Marakela's eyes lit up. "That's it! We c'n go huntin' Bloodkin! They c'd be runnin' round the country killin' folks!"

"Not likely," Baer rumbled. "They'll stay pretty close to the bases. It's all they know. An' they won't be around forever. Remember that the Slavers killed any Bloodkin babies that were girls. They'll die out, 'fore long."

"Anyway," Finn said, "the Earth has seen enough fighting

and killing to last it for a long time. Maybe forever, with luck."

"I s'pose," Marakela said gloomily. "Maybe me an' the girls'll go explorin', with Corwin an' the rest." She brightened a little. "I always wanted t'travel."

Soon afterwards, it was Finn's turn to grow restless, and to think of travel. His Wasteland friends saw it – and though the thought of his leaving was painful to them, they understood, even before he tried to explain.

"I've felt at home on the Wasteland – you know that," he told them. "But I'm still a forest creature. I need to see some real wilderness again. My kind of wilderness – back east. And now, there are no enemies to stop me."

"That goes fer me, too," Josh said. "I like the folks here real fine, but I'd be happy never t' see *sand* again in my life."

Jena sighed. "A few months ago, I was telling Finn that I'd never leave the Wasteland. But that was when there were still battles to be fought. Now I don't need to be a warrior any more, and I'm feeling like Finn is. I'd like to go home."

And so, in a while, after many more heart-wrenching farewells, a small group of riders left the main camp of the Wasteland people, and headed northeast. There were six of them – Finn and his family, and Baer, and with them Marakela and Rainshadow who were accompanying them on only the first stage of their journey. They were heading for one of the desert water-holes, the oasis near the edge of the Wasteland, where Finn and Baer had first met Rainshadow. That place of meeting was now to be their place of parting.

They rode on that journey mostly in silence, each lost in thought, re-living the memories of all the wild dangers they had shared, all the closeness they had developed. And they rode slowly, as if to put off the final moment as long as possible. But in the end, the patch of tangled green-brown foliage came into sight, and they paused by the oasis, trying to find the words they wanted to say.

"Come east some time," Jena said, "and see us." Her smile trembled. "See what a forest is like."

"Sure," Marakela said. "An' you ride this way again sometime, an' see everybody."

"We will," Finn said warmly. "We won't forget you."

"And this whole land," Rainshadow said gravely, "will never forget you, Finn Ferral – and all that has happened this past year."

Then there were tears, and handshakes, and embraces, and finally the mournful moment when the tall copper-skinned man and the big redheaded woman turned their horses, raised their hands in a silent salute, and rode away into the desert.

Finn watched them till they were out of sight, even to his hawk-eyes. Then he looked at the others with a half-smile. "Time to go," he said.

"Uh . . . Finn," Baer said, tugging at his beard uneasily. "I been thinkin'. Here you are, the three of you, a *family* again, headin' back home. So I figure . . ." His voice seemed choked, and he cleared his throat noisily. "I figure it's time for ol' Baer to say g'bye too, an' let you folks get on with your lives."

Finn's eyes were damp, but he smiled broadly. "Baer, I've been waiting a long time to say this to you." His voice deepened into a passable imitation of Baer's mellow bass. "*You're* not going anywhere, my friend. *We're* going."

Then he laughed, and the others joined in – including Baer, after a moment of amazed delight.

"You're part of this family, Baer," Jena told him.

"Wouldn't be the same without y'," Josh agreed.

"So let's get started," Finn said. "We can cover a lot of distance before nightfall."

Baer's eyes twinkled as he gave a mock-sigh. "That figures," he rumbled. "You're gonna hurry us across the country as if Slavers were still after us."

But then he sighed again, in earnest – a sigh of pure happiness, and contentment. "Leastways," he said, patting his horse's powerful neck, "we don't hafta go all the way on foot, this time."

And all four were laughing again as they urged their horses forward, and rode away across the empty sands.